Contempt
of Kourtney

NEW YORK TIMES BESTSELLING AUTHOR
EVE LANGLAIS

E-ISBN: 978 177 384 1847

Print ISBN: 978 177 384 1854

PROLOGUE ~ LUCIFER

HIS KINGDOM WAS SHRINKING, which, to a devil who had always boasted of size, proved traumatizing.

At first, he'd tried to deny it. His experts, sent to measure the ninth ring, argued. Some said the original numbers were wrong. But by the time all the groups had measured a hundred times, they couldn't deny the shrinkage. Now they argued about the cause.

"Fucking magic and mystery." He scowled. "I hate it."

"You hate a lot of things, Luc." His wife appeared, looking pale and tired. More exhausted than conditions warranted.

Yes, their two young children were a handful, but Gaia had always been a force of nature. Quite literally. Yet ever since the birth of their youngest, Jujube —a tasty little treat of a daughter who would one day cause destruction—his wife hadn't recovered. Which made no sense. The little parasite had been born, and while Gaia had been breastfeeding, she'd recently ceased, only to get worse after. Thinking the baby might have left some kind of magical parasite, he'd checked for a connection between them. Nothing. He couldn't find a single thing ailing his wife.

Day by day, his wench faded away, and it bothered him.

Appalling. He knew that. The Devil wasn't supposed to give a damn about anyone. He blamed old age for the weakness. In many ways it was more because he knew her best. They'd been through so much together. Good times. Bad times. Really fucking bad times.

They were currently in a good place. One where he—gag—cared. "You should be resting." It made his stomach churn to hear the concern in his voice, so he fixed it to a barb. "You look like shit." The honesty soured his lips. He wished for his vivacious wench who always had sunshine lighting her, hinting of green dark hair, her lips plump like ripe fruit. Now she was a haggard version of herself.

"I am aware I'm not at my best," she stated without her usual fire or glare. "I seem to be having a harder time than usual bouncing back. It doesn't help those bloody mortals keep poisoning my planet."

"I noticed they were still at it."

"And this even though I ensured a few innovative types received options for cleaning up pollution. But those activists, in their quest for a perfect solution, won't allow the most sensible fix."

"Did you really think they'd say yes to incinerators?" Truly the quickest thing they could do to reverse damage, but the activists had people convinced they would billow black smoke. False, actually.

"Personally, I was kind of partial to that fabulous microbe that eats plastic. Did you know it turns into a perfect fertilizer to rejuvenate the damage they've done?"

"It also has the potential to wipe out all life."

"It would wipe out the current life, but my world would adapt and start over again," she pointed out.

"Don't you remember how long it took the last time?" He did. He missed those dinosaurs.

"I don't want to have to wipe the slate clean, but they have to do something!" she exclaimed, finally showing a spark.

"Don't get mad at me. You're the one who whispered into all those ears to have environmental laws put in place."

"Lot of good that did." Gaia's lips turned down.

"Humans love their filth. Why do you think Heaven rejects them?" Those living in his brother's kingdom were of the opinion that most mortals

3

were a waste of space given they were stained by sin the moment of their birth.

His wife crossed her arms. "Here's to hoping they smarten up and do more than swap plastic straws for paper ones. I mean, what kind of solution is that? They're still killing my precious trees."

"Anytime you want me to start a war on Earth and enslave mankind, you let me know. I'll bludgeon them into taking care of you."

"Oh, Luc. You're too good to me." She smiled as she cupped his cheek.

In that moment, he saw his Gaia, the woman and goddess who'd obsessed him for millennia. It didn't matter they'd broken up more than a few times, dallied with others, fought and then fucked. In the end, they always came back to each other.

She rose to kiss him, her lips barely brushing his—

"Mama!"

The sudden bellow from their son didn't need a baby monitor.

"Ignore him."

The kiss lingered.

"MAMA!" The demand vibrated the walls and floor. When Junior wanted attention, it was now.

She winced. "I'll—"

He interrupted. "I've got Junior. Why don't you go lie down for a bit?"

"Sleep?" It almost seemed as if she'd refuse. She

nodded instead. "That sounds like a good idea. I'm so tired all the time. Guess at our age, maybe there's no shame in hiring someone to help with the children."

The very fact she suggested it, after being adamant they handle the raising of the pair themselves, was the direst thing he'd heard her say thus far.

"A grand idea. Let's get someone young and buxom."

"Whatever you want," she said, already fading away, off for some much-needed rest.

"Ma—"

The yell started, and Lucifer popped into the nursery before Junior could finish. He put a finger to his lips and winked at his boy.

The child, who appeared in human years around the age of two, paused in his yodel. thought about his choices for a second, and wisely chose his father with a grin and raised arms. "Da."

"I see someone isn't in need of long naps anymore." He scooped his child, enjoying the fact he didn't yet have to worry about a knife in the back.

Usually they didn't try to kill him before their teen years. He had some time yet.

A quick butt change—the dirty diaper incinerated lest the wrong sorts use it for nefarious purposes—and he tossed Junior onto his shoulders and paid a visit to his oldest daughter.

He stepped right into her new home, which she'd

chosen to make inside of Grim Dating Central, a service that was charged with pairing denizens of Hell with suitable mortals, aka fertile ones. The end goal, given his recent losses, was increasing the ranks of his legions. And since it had to do with sex, he'd offered the job to Bambi.

She'd been doing well. Too well. His daughter thrived under the challenge. He barely recognized her since she'd taken over, and it sent a chill through him. History had shown that when his children started courting power, they eventually began coveting the top demon spot.

Would Bambi be just like the rest? He'd hate to kill her. He'd almost become fond of her presence.

Finished snapping out commands, she turned to him with a smile. "Dark Lord. What a nice surprise. And how's my favorite little brother?" she cooed, blowing Junior a kiss from lips that still wore a bright red shade.

"Don't you mean your only brother?" he amended.

Turned out Christopher, the antichrist, wasn't actually his after all. Part of the reason why his slightly older sibling, Elyon, was now tucked out of sight and his son, Charlie—formerly known as Jesus —had taken charge.

"Junior knows how much I love him." Bambi held out her arms, and the boy went literally flying into them. She caught the little imp and snuggled him.

"Such a big boy. Big sis has got a treat for you in my office."

"Since when do you work behind walls?" A glance showed the open platform overlooking the room had been closed in with walls and blacked-out windows.

"Not all our applicants want it to be known they're stepping onto Earth."

"Afraid their spouses will lose their shit. Understandable."

"That and a few of them are technically banished."

"Heaven and their eternity punishments." Lucifer rolled his eyes. Even the Devil knew forever was too long for most crimes. "Do we have a plan for when Heaven finds out we are letting the permanently banned out of Hell for bootie calls with humans?" His idea. He needed minions. Humans made great incubators.

"All of our clients sign an indemnity clause and know to deny any accusations should the angels get involved. We're also interviewing some of Hell's best lawyers. The plan is to retain a few to protect us should Heaven decide to take issue."

"Excellent planning." Nothing he could bitch about. He was torn between pride in her obvious intelligence, taking after her father, and annoyance at her efficiency. Couldn't she have given him something to complain about?

He glanced around to take in the other changes. The building she worked out of was the former Canadian Reaper Guild. Bloody Canadians just wouldn't die. They lived long, and their government molly-coddled them with all kinds of laws to keep them safe. He missed the days when floating beer koozies didn't have the warning about not using them as a safety flotation device. Canadians even believed in salting their sidewalks when they were slippery. What was the point of ice if you couldn't watch someone banana peel on it?

Anyhow, those poor Canadian reapers, due to a lack of work, found themselves being reassigned to Earth working in the newly establish Grim Dating matchmaking service. Their job? To pair demons and other approved minions with fecund humans.

The operation was overseen by Bambi, and under her matchful eye, shit was starting to happen. Pregnancies were up, and morale was horny. Between this new dating operation and the Hell Cruises, he might finally see some minion growth. If his oldest daughter didn't try anything funny. She'd been strange of late.

"What happened to the disco ball?" he asked.

Last time he'd visited, the once somber guildhall had been transformed from dark stone and gloomy corners. There'd been food and drink, couples making out, and thumping music. Now the place swarmed with desks and busy minions. Seashells vibrated with messages waiting to be answered. Message bottles shot out of tubes like missiles into the hands of waiting staff. Scribes wrote as quickly as they could, ink flying from their quills, while the older school chipped at their tablets. He did see a single printer, red eyes glowing ominously as it hummed and spat out paper. A shapeshifter allowing itself to be a living machine.

If done willingly, it could only mean Bambi treated her staff well. Or perhaps he had it wrong. Could be she'd threatened the shifter into taking on that uncomfortable shape, proving she wasn't as perfect as she seemed with her ridiculously well run and organized business.

For a moment, just a moment, he wondered if the lack of chaos in what should have been a true logistical nightmare was yet another indication of the problems plaguing his realm. In normal times, there should have been minions sleeping at their desks, signs of battle or slovenliness. Disrespect around every corner.

The order was unnatural, and he left the humming hive of productivity for Bambi's office. Only it wasn't the hoped-for respite. It was yet another sign of how things had changed. The pink boudoir he'd recalled from before had been replaced with an office fit for an Earth-side executive.

Bookcases lined the walls, filled with folders organized by color. A massive desk had an inbox that was almost empty and an outbox that had a tidy stack. No computer, though. They had a tendency to glitch in Hell.

She swept a hand to one of two straight-backed chairs in front of her desk.

As if.

Lucifer ignored them and conjured a stool that perched him higher than her when she sat behind the desk with Junior on her lap.

"You've been redecorating."

"Just making the best use of my space. Who knew simple lines would be so appealing."

Lucifer almost shuddered. He hated anything too straight. Roads, rivers, walls. In Hell, everything possessed a curve. Even his framed art. "You're talking crazy."

"Am I?" She plopped Junior on her desk and leaned over to open a drawer. She pulled out a cookie and dangled it in front of Junior.

Lucifer almost lunged to bat it out of the way. What if it were poisoned? Sibling rivalry ran strong in his line. Junior was too small to realize he couldn't trust anyone. Not even family.

But acting was caring. Showing it revealed a weakness. He feigned casualness as he said, "Don't let his mother catch you. She doesn't want him eating junk food."

"Isn't a sister allowed to spoil?" Her gaze held his for a second too long before she focused on her brother. She cooed, "Who wants one of those evil cookies the Americans are so fond of?" Everyone talked about them as if they were as addictive as crack.

They were. Lucifer kept a vault full of the cookies that will not be named to use as leverage.

Junior gnawed happily. He didn't begin thrashing or choking. He lived and was content for the moment. Perhaps he should procure a stash of cookies to save the outfits the boy liked chewing and slobbering on. A teething baby was nothing to mock.

"How may I serve you today, Dark Lord?" Such respect. Where were the saucy retorts? The rudeness? Bambi waited patiently for his reply.

Ack. "We have a problem," he said.

"I hear the ninth ring appears to be shrinking."

"A temporary setback." He waved a hand. He expected he'd find a way to fix it when he had the time to pay it more mind. He always did. "The calamity we have involves my wife."

Too late he caught the many problems with that statement. First off using "we." In his world, it should always be "I." Me and myself also being acceptable. Second, he'd shown concern for a specific entity. He knew better than to show preference for someone. It would make Gaia a target for his enemies. Although, to be fair, as Mother Earth, she dealt with her fair share of attacks already.

"Don't you know how to make your wife *happy*?"

Just that one inflected word and yet he eyed Bambi sharply. "Are you implying something?" As if anyone could ever doubt his prowess in that respect. He'd invented sex. Every perversion? Him. All him.

"I would never imply anything, Dark Lord." She gazed back, attentive and obedient.

It was wrong. So utterly fucking wrong. The Devil's children rarely remained loyal. A part of him screamed to not forget his past, reminded him he should never trust. Yet, in this instance, he needed to delegate. Too many things required specialized attention, and he knew better than to clone himself. He'd seen the movie. The original perished and the clone took his place.

Since he couldn't do everything, he had to parcel out some tasks. "Something is ailing Gaia."

"She did just birth two remarkable children in short order. She's probably still recovering. Perhaps she's experiencing some postpartum issues?" Bambi uttered the right amount of concern and the perfect reply. Was she fucking with him, or did she not take him seriously?

"It's more than that. It's as if something is draining her strength."

"I know the climate on the mortal plane has been somewhat erratic lately, but I hear the efforts to govern pollution are growing in popularity."

He shook his head as he pushed off the stool to pace. "No. She's had problems with that before."

Volcanoes erupting, spilling molten rock and ash for hundreds of miles. The dark and middle ages, where sewage ran down the streets. "All those previous poisons never made her sick. Something is wrong."

"Is it magical?"

"No." He'd checked and checked.

"No injuries? Maybe internal?"

He shook his head.

"Ever think it's just exhaustion because she's not as young as she used to be? If you ask me, you're probably worrying about nothing."

The very fact she placated him only exacerbated the feeling he was missing something. Something crucial. Which was why, when he left the guild, he dropped Junior off with Pokie—a former Atlantean and most excellent major domo—to make sure he got some lunch then set up a meeting in his office.

Unfortunately, his best spy had recently gotten hooked up with his middle child, Muriel. She now had five husbands, and rumor said she was courting a female as her sixth spouse. He'd be proud if he weren't so jealous.

He had to rely on the services of his third best spy given his second, Teivel, was also giving it to his daughter. Was his daughter doing it on purpose to take away his best soldiers? He'd hate to have to kill a few of them to temper her growing power.

At least he could count on Noel to not leave him. The vampire was about as joyful as a Christmas tree set on fire and then pissed on to put out. Yet, for all her dourness, she had excellent skulking skills.

He didn't need to explain himself, just say, "There's a traitor at the Canuck guild. Find them and who they're reporting to."

"Yes, Dark Lord."

Within the hour, Noel was watching the former Canadian reaper guildhall. Being the loyal sort, she kept him apprised as she followed a rather benign imp who left, looking entirely too casual according to her. Unlike most imps, her target didn't beeline for the nearest tavern. Rather it fled stealthily, weaving into the many alleys of that ring and the next, as if trying to lose anyone that might follow.

As if Noel could be so easily lost. She kept on that imp's tail and reported right up to the point where the imp disappeared into a cave in the seventh ring that hadn't been inhabited for a very long time. The previous dung beetle owner had hoarded poop and left behind quite a mess.

The vampire tracker lingered outside the cave.

"What's inside?" Lucifer asked, talking to Noel via the compact mirror he used for scrying afar with minions on a mission. Not that he actually saw her. Noel chose to be a classic vampire. No reflection whatsoever but he could hear her voice.

"Judging by the many tracks going in and few coming out, I would hypothesize a portal, Dark

Lord." She had the proper somber respect for her master.

"An illegal one going where?" he mused aloud. There were more than a few planes, none of which really welcomed demons. Only Earth kind of tolerated them, but again, only so long as they followed the terms of the treaty with Heaven. And demons were supposed to ask for permission to go Earthside.

"Would my dark lord like me to investigate?"

"Yes! Get your ass in there, find out where the imp has gone." She entered the portal, but never reported back in. The cops found her mirror in an alley.

Who dared meddle with Lucifer's minion? Someone would pay.

1

USING his cloak to hide in shadows, Dwayne skulked outside a building with a flashing sign: Live Dancers. It also boasted a pumping fast techno beat. He'd wager there were strobe lights inside and crowded sweaty bodies, bumping and grinding.

The very idea he might have to enter the dance club made his shadow shiver. For one, inside meant people.

He hated people.

For another, they weren't just people but humans.

He didn't like humans.

Even though he didn't need a third reason, he had one. An intense dislike of parties. All that frantic joy and laughter.

If he had a choice, he would be lounging in his new home—an apartment with way more space than he was used to. He'd gone a little overboard decorating. He'd gotten a big fat chair, a giant screen TV, and a king-sized mattress for sleeping. Pure luxury compared to his tiny cell-like room and straw-stuffed pallet at the old reaper guild.

If he was home, he could be watching the fights or listening to Joe Rogan. Problem with listening to Joe was the craving for a joint. He didn't do that shit anymore. He remembered all too well the relaxation that turned to paranoia and had him sitting with his back pressed against a wall, holding a gun in his lap.

The good ol' days before he started working for the Devil as a reaper. But today, he wasn't seeking someone's dying soul. His was a secret mission that only he and his commander, Brody, knew of.

Find a missing vampire, a task he was well better suited for than his current employment for Grim Dating. For months since his reassignment from a reaper to Date Location Scout for Grim Dating, he'd been demanding a transfer to another guild. He missed the old days of reaping. Nothing appearing as a looming, ominous force that frightened the dead into following him to Hell. He craved the rush of chasing down a fleeing spirit who thought it could escape justice. None ever escaped his long scythe or his stern glare as he told them to behave or else.

But did all his previous accomplishments save

him from the shame of working for what amounted to little more than a brothel?

It was only by luck that he'd managed to skip actually dealing with people in person. His skills didn't lay with the actual matchmaking but rather the scouting of potential locations for clients and human prospects to meet. Mermaid who could appear like a human woman, but needed sex in the water? Filched keys and alarm code meant they could arrange after-hour fun at a recreation center.

A demon whose inner temperature ran a little too hot? How about a make-out session in a freezer?

Specialized locations weren't the only thing he had to handle. At times, he also assisted in coordinating events with extraction teams. Misbehaving demons who didn't get proper permission before tupping humans, or those that thought they could flee their very limited time on Earth, found themselves dragged back to Hell to face punishment. Chasing them down almost fluffed his reaper robe.

Would he get to run someone down tonight?

Maybe the vampire he'd been sent to find. Name of Noel. Dark hair. Pale skin. No picture because she was of the nonreflecting variety. Which made his only clue ironic.

A mirror. Apparently, she'd been carrying one when she came over to the mortal plane. It was discovered in an alley beside the club he currently watched. A club that appeared quite mundane.

Humans going in. Humans going out.

He could see the appeal for a vampire, though. Drunk people often times had no issue sliding into an alley for some necking that might leave a hickey.

While the commander hadn't said so in as many words, Dwayne got the impression harm had befallen the vampire. Whereas Dwayne, who took cynicism to a new level, assumed she'd seen an opening to flee Hell's grip and took it.

Only ornery old bastards like him preferred living in the underworld to topside. At least in Hell he could be as miserable as he liked and no one said shit to him. Those on this plane of existence expected him to smile, be pleasant, be courteous.

Not putting his foot up annoying asses was being kind.

Wrapping his cloak around himself, he stood watch. Only the walking dead rushed in. He took his time, tracked the many souls—all human—entering.

He'd begun to think he'd wasted his time when, around the two a.m. mark, he felt it. A disturbance that permeated the air and grew stronger until a car stopped in front of the club. Then it was if time stood still. The few humans outside having ciga-rettes didn't pay any mind as the door closest to the sidewalk opened. A hooded figure emerged, its silver cape long and still, not the living dark undulation worn by reapers.

From where Dwyane watched, he couldn't tell

what hid under the hood, but he'd wager his left testicle it wasn't human. Which made this a clue.

The figure glided into the club, past the bouncer who not once even looked their way.

Time to follow. Dwyane shoved away from the wall, and his cloak shifted out of sight as he stomped across the road to the club entrance. Hiding was all well and good when there were shadows. Inside a crowded club, walking into the unknown, best to act mundane.

The doorman opened his mouth as if he'd say something.

"Don't." Dwayne glared.

It should be noted he'd perfected his glare since his death more than forty years before. It helped he was six feet and half, wide as a linebacker, and in no mood for bullshit. Get in his way and he would move you. Not nicely and with no guarantee of living when he was done.

The doorman wisely stepped aside. He would live another day. Dwayne entered the club, and it was his worst nightmare. Strobing lights neon illuminated everywhere from the lime green couches to the brighter orange floor. Hot pinks. Sizzling blues. It was as if nature had vomited a psychedelic rainbow. It attracted humans in the same kinds of colors along with white that caught the black lights.

It was enough to give anyone seizures. But even more annoying was the crowd.

He bunched his body and barreled in. His size should have deterred the humans from touching him. Instead it was if they were drawn by his rigid nature. Sweaty fingers ran along his biceps, pinched his ass. If he didn't know the trouble he'd get in, he would have slapped a few hands. Snapped a wrist or two. Knocked together some heads.

But that would make the commander angry. Then he'd get another lecture on how humans were fragile. Blah. Blah. Blah.

Dwayne was fully aware of their fragility and how he wasn't on the mortal plane to take lives. Every now and then he couldn't help himself and reaped a deserving soul. He immediately reported his crime to the commander and declared himself ready to return to Hell as punishment. Instead, he got sent to sensitivity training.

The teacher almost died. Mostly because he got Dwayne to explore his feelings. Real men didn't do that kind of weird shit. Who cared if he had anxiety. And a bit of depression. No, he wasn't getting a fucking cat. Or dog. Or the most awful suggestion of all from the teacher, a girlfriend. He did not need that kind of annoyance in his life.

The hand cupping his groin led to him peeling it off and glaring down at the woman with sparkly dusted eyes. She smiled, the ring through her lower lip catching the lights. She mouthed, "Wanna fuck?"

Before his death, she was exactly the type he

would have said yes to. One-night stand, no strings. Hell, he'd barely remember anything the next day after a night spent partying.

He didn't miss that hollow existence. He thrust her hand from him and strode away without answering.

Since he didn't see a sign of the hooded person, he headed for the bar. New arrivals tended to gravitate to a drink. His gaze scanned those waiting for beverages. He didn't see signs of the cloak.

At his approach, people scattered, and Dwayne slapped the countertop.

The bartender, his lips slathered in sparkles to match his eyes, mouthed, "Beer?"

Everyone always assumed, because of his size and appearance, he drank lager. Again, that would be the old Dwayne. New Dwayne didn't drink at all.

He mouthed, "Water."

The bartender wrinkled his nose. Shook his head. Held up a finger. He then proceeded to do some fancy dance that involved a glass and various shots of liquid, finished with liquid smoke.

With a flourish, the bartender presented it to Dwayne.

It was the height of absurdity. He should have just said yes to the beer. It wasn't as if he would drink it. It was merely to serve as a prop to help him blend in. As if that were possible. It wasn't just his size that set him apart.

He waded through the hyper crowd, making his way across the vast room. At one time, there might have been walls, but now tall metal columns rose in strategic spots to support the ceiling, mini ledges ringing them at just the right height to place drinks or casually lean to watch the crowd.

The two guys who'd staked out the best spot in the place didn't need much glaring to decide they wanted to move. Dwayne rested the drink on the shelf, leaned his back against the support, and surveilled the room once more.

No sign of a robe, but then again, they might have shed it upon coming inside, which meant he should instead be seeking that sense of otherness. Surely, he could spot the non-human in the place.

Wrong.

They snuck up on him.

It was only instinct that had him whirling to behold his target. The hood was pushed back to reveal platinum hair that absorbed the colored lights rather than reflected them. The features were fine, the lips full. The split in her cloak showed she wore a dress that molded her shape.

"Hello, reaper." The words held a feminine lilt and could be heard quite easily despite the noise.

"My name is Dwayne." A dumb way of skirting the fact she saw right through his mundane disguise.

"And I am Raella."

"You're not human," he stated.

"I should hope not." Her nose wrinkled. "Look at them." She gestured to the dancing crowd. "Like simple-minded moths, bashing around, desperate for something to make them feel before they die."

"You make it sound as if they're unhappy."

"Aren't they?" She waved her hand. "Drunk. Stoned. Partying hard to forget their miserable lives."

"Can you blame them? Being human sucks. After all, we're born damned. We die damned. And then have an eternity to regret our bad choices."

"Do you have regrets, Dwayne?"

"Too many to count."

"Why are you here?"

"Why all the questions?"

"Can't a girl be curious?" She tried batting her lashes and failed at innocence. It only highlighted her conniving nature.

"Who are you?"

"Forgotten my name already?"

"I haven't, *Raella*," he stressed. "Maybe the right question would be, *what* are you?"

Perfect pearly teeth emerged as she smiled. "That kind of answer requires privacy where the simple-minded won't interrupt. But first." She leaned over him, her hand brushing over his as she snatched his glass of alcohol. The froth on it had settled, and now it simply glowed. For all he knew it contained something radioactive.

The strange female tossed it back and licked her lips, the tip of her tongue pink and normal looking. Everything about her was just right from her perfectly sloped nose to her fine brows to her smooth skin.

She grinned. "Shall we go somewhere we can talk?" She didn't wait for a reply. Her cape swished at her back as she led the way.

He followed and waited until they were in the alley before she stopped and clasped her hands. "We're alone now. Ask your questions, reaper."

"What are you?"

"That's not the right question."

"It's a basic one, which you're dodging."

"Because it's boring. Let's go to the next one," she suggested. "Why am I here."

"That's obvious, to cause trouble. Do you have permission from Hell's Immigration Services to visit this plane?"

"Do I look like someone who spends time in the Underworld?" Her grimace twisted her lips.

"You're not from Earth."

"How can you tell?"

He stared at her. "You have no soul."

That rounded her mouth. "There are many without souls on this planet."

"None of them are native to it. Those born on Earth, even the smallest of insects, has a speck of soul."

"Do you miss owning yours, reaper? Do you regret bargaining your soul into the Dark Lord's service?"

"No." He quite honestly knew he'd made the right choice. "Are we done playing word games? I need you to answer some questions."

"And what if I don't want to answer?"

"Then I will pull rank. Consider yourself notified that I am declaring myself an emissary of Hell, on special mission for the Dark Lord himself. You will cooperate or be reported to Hell's Delinquency Bureau for obstruction."

"We wouldn't want that," was her coy reply. "Ask your questions, reaper, and I will do my best to answer."

He doubted it, but he started anyway. "Have you seen a vampire recently?"

"You'll have to be more specific. I've seen many in the last month. This is, after all, New Orleans. There's something about the graveyards that attracts them."

"Short bobbed hair. Serious expression. Last known location was just outside this club."

"Was her name Noel?"

Too easy but he played along. "Yes. Do you know her current location?"

"I do. And even better, I can bring you to her." She grabbed for his hand before he could snatch it away.

Her fingers were cold. Too cold for the outside temperature. She squeezed hard enough his bones shifted. If he wanted to, he could have shifted his hand into shadow, but that would be admitting discomfort.

He held in his grimace and said, "No need to cling like an ex-girlfriend who can't let go. Lead the way. I'll follow."

"So eager. Slow down. In my day, things weren't always in a rush. Men knew how to take their time," she stated, tightening her grip and cracking the bones.

He tried to dissipate his hand but failed. The flutter of fabric shadow as his cloak reacted was the only betrayal of his agitation. "Release my hand."

"I will. When I'm done with it," she hissed just as she dug her nails into the flesh, the stabs burning pinpricks.

He pulled, but she held tight, and as he stared at her, the shimmering hair also appeared dark, absorbing all the light. The whites of her eyes bled into purple, the same hue as her iris. Her lips parted over sharp, pointed teeth.

Not human, and dangerous.

His jaw tightened. No more being courteous. His free hand flexed and then closed around a familiar haft. Some reapers were old school with the scythes. Some, like Derrick, enjoyed the lightness and versatility of a bat.

Dwayne swung the axe.

Or meant to. The thing gripping him hissed, dug its nails deeper, and oblivion rushed to greet him.

The next thing he knew, he woke to shouts of, "Hands where we can see them!" and no idea whose blood covered him.

2

KOURTNEY BARELY HAD time to skim the online news headlines, taking a few seconds to read the one labeled, *Blood Bath in the Club District*. The article painted a grisly picture with the only highlight being they'd caught the killer. Although she'd wager they'd hold off laying charges until they found a body. If the accused managed to get a competent lawyer, that was. Not too long ago, that would have been her trying.

As a former public defender, she remembered all too well the low salary, long hours, and little to no job satisfaction. She'd spent the last decade since graduating law school getting sentences reduced or even tossed out. On track for a promotion. If she had a dick.

Being passed over for someone younger, with less experience and a horrible track record, had led to her snapping and calling out the toxic male culture in her workplace. All true, and yet the attitude toward her afterwards, even from those who would benefit her calling it out, meant she resigned.

She deserved better. Problem being she didn't exactly have clients knocking on her door—possibly because she didn't have a public office yet, just one in her house. Luckily, her three clients tended to meet her at the jailhouse on account they were repeat offenders.

They'd heard she quit the public defender's office and insisted she be the one to handle their cases. But she needed more than three career criminals to keep her afloat, hence the upcoming interview.

A newly established dating service was seeking full-time legal representation. She didn't hold much hope she'd get the contract. As a newly minted law firm with only criminal experience and exactly one employee—*Me!*—chances were the company would choose someone bigger, more established. She didn't exactly come with a glowing recommendation. Just a forthright attitude and her record, which was pretty darned good.

While she might be convinced she didn't stand a chance, she wasn't a coward to shy away from trying. Adversity was a close friend. She'd not made it through a rough childhood and sleepless years at college to give up now.

This might be the luck she'd dreamed of. After

all, it was a wonder she'd even heard about Grim Dating's search for representation. The anonymous email sent to her address—with the return address of darklord69 at hell dot com—was an obvious spoof, and yet when she called Grim Dating to ask if they were actually looking for a lawyer, it checked out. She received an appointment to meet the owners of the company, Brody Reaper and Posie Ringwald. Only recent partners, according to what she'd gleaned.

The Lyft service deposited her on the sidewalk outside the offices of Grim Dating. The company took up an entire multi-floor building, a modern concrete affair with mirror-like windows. As she approached the front doors, she noticed a scaffold holding workers installing a coffin-shaped sign. It featured a cartoon grim reaper with a scythe stabbing a heart. It didn't exactly scream romance to her, but entering the bustling building through sliding glass doors, she had to admit they at least gave the appearance of being successful.

She strode across the gray tile floor, back straight, chin up. She'd learned at an early age to always appear as if she belonged. Hesitation would get her thrown out.

A security guard slouching at a desk perked up at the sight of her. "Excuse me, ma'am. Can I help you? Are you here for an interview?"

"Yes. I have a two p.m. appointment." She was ten minutes early. She hated being late.

"Your name?"

"Kourtney Blake."

He frowned as he eyed his list. He ran his finger down the clipboard, flipped the page, then back. "I'm not seeing your name. Perhaps you got the date wrong? Do you know the name of the Grim match-maker you're supposed to meet?"

"Mr. Reaper and Ms. Ringwald's secretary made the appointment with me. I assumed I would be meeting with them."

"You have an appointment with the commander and his lady?" His brows rose. "Wait a second, you're not here for a dating interview, are you?"

Her tone turned frosty. "Most certainly not." Relationships were for those without student debt who didn't mind catering to the needs of someone else. She had little patience or time for that. She'd not spent all those years in college to give up her career and pop out babies. "I'm here because your company is in need of legal representation."

"Well shit. A lady lawyer." He seemed flabber-gasted. "Women sure have come a long way, eh?"

Detailing the many ways he came off as sexist and opened himself up for a lawsuit for discrimina-tion probably wouldn't help her get the job, so she held her tongue and instead said, "We're even allowed to drive cars." Okay, so she couldn't stem the sarcasm entirely.

"Wonders will never cease." The guard shook his head, more bemused than rude, as if it truly were a strange thing to him.

She hoped the entire company wouldn't have the same attitude. She'd left one testosterone-driven environment and wasn't about to suffer another.

The elevator took her to the top floor, where the guard assured her someone would direct her to the right office.

Upon exiting the cab, she was struck again by the prosperous appearance of the place. Lots of chrome and spanking new carpet and paint. Everything done in shades of gray.

The vestibule held a massive round counter, behind which a lady with fat sausage-curled hair sat, wearing cat-eye glasses that had a chain hanging from each arm. Her red lips pursed at the sight of her.

"The interviews with the matchmaking reps are on the first floor," she snottily stated.

Apparently, the attitude with the guard wasn't restricted to just the males. "I've got an appointment with Mr. Reaper and Ms. Ringwald."

"You're K. Blake?" She looked down at her desk then up again. "It didn't mention you were a mundane female."

"Is that a problem?" was her cool reply. "You do

realize that discrimination on the basis of gender is an indictable offense."

The woman behind the counter smiled wider than seemed normal. "At least you're not a pushover. Still, I can't see how you can help. You're ill equipped to handle our kinds of cases."

"I don't think that's your call to make. Now, might I suggest you do your job and inform your employer I am here for my interview."

"Suit yourself." The woman leaned down as she pressed some buttons on her phone, her voice barely a whisper.

Since there was nowhere to sit, Kourtney stood and waited. Not long as it turned out.

The rude receptionist curled her lip as she said, "They'll see you now. Through there." She pointed to the door farthest from them.

The sign on it read CEO with a pink sticky note beside it adding an S. It appeared one of the pair she was meeting might be new.

Upon entering, she discovered yet another reception area, this time with a couch and table sporting magazines. Behind the desk, a handsome man, his hair dark, his skin tan, his smile wide as he swung his feet off the surface. "So you're the lawyer. You must be something considering the recommendation you got."

"The public defender's office supplied you with one?" She couldn't help the surprise in her voice.

He started and eyed her more closely. Then muttered, "Oh shit. I think there's been a mistake." He glanced down at his desk, which held a scrap of yellowed paper, then her. "You are K. Blake?"

"Yes," she snapped a little tersely. "And I realize I'm not a man and not what you expected. Are you Mr. Reaper?"

"No. I'm Julio. I work for him." He scrubbed a hand through his hair. "Listen, miss, I think there's been a mistake."

"It's *Ms.* Blake, and I'm here to interview with Mr. Reaper and Ms. Ringwald." Spoken firmly and hinting at her annoyance. "I wouldn't suggest you interfere any further with my attempt to gain employment, or you will find yourself in a very uncomfortable legal situation."

"Just trying to help." He sighed. "Suit yourself." He rolled out of his chair with fluid grace and stuck his head through yet another door, speaking low enough she couldn't hear.

It wasn't long before he waved her through, and she finally found herself in an office befitting the CEO of a successful company. More chrome and gray carpet, but the view from the extensive windows was the real showstopper.

She didn't pay it much mind though, more interested by the people inside.

Behind a massive desk sat a man in a dark suit. Not just dark, black. More suited to a mortician than a dating guru. By his side, wearing a striking red business ensemble consisting of a blouse, jacket, and pencil skirt, was a woman, which did much to alleviate her concerns. Surely a company that gave them equal CEO footing would give Kourtney a fair shot.

She didn't wait but took the first step. "Thank you for meeting with me."

"This must be a joke," huffed the man she knew from pictures to be Brody Reaper.

"Be nice," hissed Ms. Ringwald. She smiled at her. "Please excuse him. He's having a bad day. I am very pleased to meet you. You come highly recommended."

Again, with that comment. Had someone actually given her a glowing review? "You'll find I am well versed in criminal matters and have dealt quite a bit with family court too." Career criminals didn't always make for great parents. Imagine that.

"Which you achieved with excellent results when working for the government and all the access and benefits that entails," Mr. Reaper pointed out.

He still seemed angry, and it put her on the defensive. Because he did have a point. "I realize that you might have been looking for a larger team to handle your affairs. However, I assure you, I know who to hire if delegation is required to get the job done."

"Even more outsiders." The man drummed his fingers impatiently.

"Her record is most impressive," Ms. Ringwald said in an aside.

"For a human," was what she could have sworn she heard the man mutter.

"We have our orders." Ringwald made the odd remark before smiling at Kourtney. "How soon can you start?"

Could it be so simple? Had she gotten the job? "Anytime. Why? Do you have a pressing legal concern for me to handle?" How bad could it be? She imagined they made their clients sign contracts to prevent indemnity. But then again, they'd been seeking a criminal lawyer. Had a client gotten a little rough on a date?

Ringwald spoke slowly. "As a matter of fact, we do have an item that requires careful and yet immediate handling. It seems an employee of ours has been arrested by accident."

"Charged with what?" she asked.

"Murder."

3

DWAYNE REPLAYED his early morning arrest over in his mind, no closer to understanding what happened.

Things hadn't gotten any better since the cop had said, "Hands where I can see them."

"What the fuck is going on?" He couldn't help slurring his words and blinking as he tried to grasp what was happening.

"Are you seriously going to play stupid?" scoffed the officer, his bulletproof vest straining over his midsection. He held his gun out, no finger on the trigger, but it wouldn't take much to set him off. "Take a look around you."

"Someone appears to have spilled their Bloody Mary." Dwayne played stupid. No way would he admit he knew this was blood. He'd tasted the coppery tang in the air and recognized it even if something about it seemed off.

"You know that ain't no drink," huffed the cop with the nametag of Smith. The lush mustache above his lip twitched.

Envy filled him at the sight of it. He never did have much luck with the facial hair. He managed a patchy scruff at best.

"What is it? Ketchup?" Dwayne asked, even as he stared at the red hands he held over his head. It was as if he'd buried his arms to the elbow in someone's oozing body.

"The blood of whoever you killed." Agitated, the younger cop took a step closer. Just a little closer and it wouldn't take much to grab hold of him.

Smith noticed and cautioned his eager partner. "Back up, Ricky. We don't know if he's armed."

"Exactly who are you accusing me of murdering? I don't see a body." Even more interesting, he saw no signs of damage. Glasses still sat on the bar, the mirrors and bottles behind it intact.

"Tell us who you killed," barked the young Ricky who ignored his partner's advice and inched closer, the grip on his weapon sweaty and twitchy. Not long out of the academy. Still flinching at every perceived threat. It wouldn't take much to set him off.

"I don't fucking know." Thinking only served to aggravate the pounding in his head. Noise. Color. It overwhelmed. "I think I should lie down."

He could barely hold his head up, so he didn't bother and eyed the floor. Pale orange cement and, jutting from it, the metal pillars with their shelves of glasses and garbage. The club from the night before appeared remarkably less impressive when illuminated. A Cinderella turned into a bare hovel. Empty compared to last night.

The fog began to thin, and clarity returned. He took stock of the situation, scanning left to right. No cameras that he could see, just the young officer and, a few paces behind, the older cop, Smith, who'd yet to say anything. His hand rested on the grip of his weapon.

No patrons. No body. So how could they accuse him of a crime?

"Are you sure someone died?" he asked. A perfectly valid question given the circumstances.

The asshole cop replied, "Hands up!"

Given he'd barely lowered them, he glared instead. A human threatening him?

He could feel his cloak rippling, ready to come at his command and give him an advantage against the guns. Nasty weapons. They kept the reapers busy. Some guns were so prolific that a reaper was attached to it permanently. The massacres they could accomplish sometimes had the reapers working in teams to collect souls. Most of the time, though, death was a solitary thing, and they worked alone.

Two humans. Easy enough to handle. First, subdue them and then flip over to headquarters to get that handy spell that could wipe a few hours of memory. The officers would awake not knowing what they'd seen. Their minds a blank.

Blank...

Hold on a second. Even his fuzzy mind latched onto the idea that maybe he'd been doped! It would explain why the fuck he couldn't remember a thing. Never mind the fact he didn't know if that was possible. The facts fit.

Someone roofied his ass!

Speaking of which... He glanced down. Fully dressed in the same clothes as last night with no evidence of having removed them. Unmolested it would seem but being framed. It was so obvious. As if he would ever kill so messily and allow himself to be caught.

"I'm going to ask you to get on your knees, hands on top of your head," demanded the young kid. He danced almost in place, shifting and leaning and shifting again. He couldn't stand still, but his gun never wavered. It remained on Dwayne, daring him to make a wrong move.

Given in solid form he could be damaged, he'd have to take care of the gun first. He also needed to remember to call in a clean team to handle the scene. The commander wouldn't be happy.

As he was about to act, more police officers burst

onto the scene, screaming, "Hands where we can see them." And wouldn't you know, they appeared to be wearing body cameras, watching every move he made.

Fuck.

Turning into the invisible man in front of them would draw attention. And that was the number one rule they weren't supposed to break.

Fucking hell.

Dwayne remained on his knees and placed his hands on his head.

One of the arriving reinforcements exclaimed, "Holy fuck, he's covered in blood."

Quite a bit of it. Someone must have poured it on him because he didn't have the battle wounds of someone who'd killed a person. No sore joints or scraped knuckles. Nothing under his nails. Swinging his axe would have tugged at the muscles in his arms and upper shoulders.

If he'd not actually gone on a rampage, then his next best hypothesis was that he'd passed out. Which jived more with his final recollection of entering a noisy bar and walking around with a drink.

Then nothing.

"What's your name?"

"Dwayne Johnston."

"Ha. Funny guy. As if anyone is going to mistake you for the Rock."

He gritted his jaw. "I said. John-ston. Check my wallet if you don't believe me."

Blending in meant having proper ID. What he didn't count on was the annoyance of having a name so similar to the famous actor and wrestling star. More than once he'd shown his appreciation of a particularly annoying remark—with his fist.

"Someone get a camera and specimen bags over here. We need to take samples."

The police quickly moved to secure the scene, which included him. He wore their evidence, and that appeared to confuse them. A few muttered something about they better not ruin the chain of evidence or the new DA would have them written up again. They argued over whether Dwayne should strip there—before he dirtied the back of their car—or the station. No one had any clothes for him, none that would fit, and as they were reminded by the commanding officer in charge, they'd better go by the book so nothing got tossed.

While they argued about it, he stood within view of where he'd woken. Yellow markers were placed next to the bloody scuffs and tacky pools. Look there was his handprint. And that dent in the drying puddle? Soaked up by the knees on his jeans. All kinds of evidence tying him to the scene.

He looked guilty. Didn't matter if he had done it or not; it had been staged to make sure he took the blame. He was ruined. His cover useless now. It would get him tossed out of the company for sure.

He almost smiled. At last, he could go home. To Hell. Giving up his television, which he had to admit he'd miss, along with jogs at sunset and that hot dog stand with the cheese and bacon sauce.

The reminder of things he'd miss brought a frown. Since when did Hell suck in comparison to Earth? He liked the ashy plane with the hustling and bustling that came with billions living in less space than the world currently had.

Could it be he'd preferred it because he'd forgotten the pleasures of living a mortal life?

That or he was going soft. A good thing he'd soon be returning to where he belonged.

He held out his hands to be bagged. Did they plan to remove them for analysis? And how many pictures did they need of his scowl?

Many humans droned on and on, asking him what happened then got annoyed when he yawned. He couldn't help it. They bored him, and from there, it didn't take long for him to become impatient.

The humans thought they could detain him? A reaper? As if he had time for their petty laws.

Play their game. He could almost hear the commander talking to him. The humans had all kinds of rights for the person being arrested. He would know since this wasn't the first time he'd gotten into trouble. The last time he'd been reported for smacking someone and he was charged with aggravated assault. How about a counter charge of aggravating him? The demon he'd been sent to collect knew he'd misbehaved. Deserved the punch to the face.

The only reason Dwayne ended up released that time was because the so-called victim claimed they'd suffered a misunderstanding and the witness recanted. He knew he wouldn't get off that easily this time.

He was taken to police headquarters where they took his fingerprints and his picture. He didn't resist. Didn't do a damned thing at all. His briefing before coming over to the mortal plane had been clear. In order to maintain a presence here, they were to obey the laws. Act human. And if arrested, keep your mouth shut and ask for your phone call.

While there was grumbling, the cops knew they couldn't deny it. Someone handed him a cellphone. While only recently arrived on this plane, everyone knew the commander's number.

Of course, using it before dawn meant it was answered with a barked, "What the fuck is so important it couldn't wait?"

Leaning against a cement block wall, knowing there were eyes watching and electronic devices probably listening, he kept it succinct. "I was arrested. They're saying I murdered someone."

The commander didn't immediately reply. And

when he did, it was to say only, "Say nothing. Demand to speak to your lawyer."

"I don't have one."

"I know. But it will stall them while I line one up."

Stalling meant he got led to an interview room, where he crossed his arms and refused to speak except to repeat, "I want my lawyer."

"Who is your lawyer?"

"They'll be here soon."

Not the reply the cops wanted. It was a few hours before they finally let him leave that windowless room. He'd hoped for some food. Instead he got a room with communal showers.

A pair of cops watched him. One being his crime scene pal Ricky, who sneered as he said, "Take it off, big boy."

That drew a stare from him.

"You do it, or I do it. I don't think you want the latter." The bigger officer, last name on his badge Harris, had a hand on a Taser.

Dwayne almost dared him to do it. He would steal the electric weapon and turn it on its owner. Then…what? Take out the other cop and escape against orders?

The commander said to stall. He eyed the dirty tile sloping to a drain. Time for the charade to end. So what if they had a file on him? His name was a creation. A fake.

The Grim crew would scrub his apartment and

move someone in to mask the fact he used to live there. He'd cease to exist. They might have his picture, but they wouldn't be able to find him. Not until they died and crossed over. Maybe he'd be the one to reap their souls.

"I think he wants me to help," said Ricky.

"I'm going to help you to an early grave if you touch me," Dwayne warned.

He tugged his cloak, his shadow, his shield—it didn't respond. Not even a whisper of movement. Which had him craning to eye the tops of his shoulders then his back. The robe still hung from him, invisible to the human eye unless he chose to show it. He gripped the toggles on each side holding it on his body. The tiny skull buttons appeared intact. So why didn't the cloak respond to his command?

Could it be a residual effect of whatever drug he got hit with? Whatever the case, it couldn't help him escape, and the young cop reached out to touch him.

He grabbed him by the wrist before it connected and growled, "I wouldn't do that."

Something in Dwayne's eyes must have changed Ricky's mind because he swallowed hard as he said, "I'm the one in charge."

"Are you?" he drawled, squeezing tight enough to grind bone.

The other cop clicked his Taser to draw attention. "Let go of Ricky and get undressed. Put your clothes in here." Harris held out a plastic bag.

"Do you have clothes for me to put on after?" he asked.

Ricky grumbled but soon returned with a two-piece prison outfit large enough to fit. "Fucking diva." He tossed it on the floor.

"Now turn around."

"You ashamed, big boy?" Ricky said, only to catch Dwayne's gaze and finish with, "You got exactly one minute." He pivoted, as did the other cop, who sidled close to whisper.

They didn't trust him and planned to attack with the Taser when he was vulnerable in the water. Attack with electricity. He knew who that ended badly for.

Dwayne stripped out of the stiff garments. They were ruined, and he found he actually looked forward to the cleansing heat of the shower. In Hell, running water wasn't a guarantee. Issues in the piping system happened all the time. From fat bergs to mutant hell rats, they could make a simple thing like water for cleaning seem like the biggest luxury.

He stood under the tepid spray, letting it stream past his cheeks, wondering if a good shower would wake up his robe. Because he really wasn't keen on putting on the scratchy prison outfit.

And then rescue arrived.

4

"WHO THE FUCK ARE YOU?" exclaimed Harris.

No one replied, but the overpowering scent of a field full of burning flowers permeated the room.

Dwayne whirled to see both cops slumped on the floor, and the Dark Lord standing over them, wearing a wig and a frothy green dress, of all things.

"Er, my lord?" He couldn't help but question even as he dipped to a knee.

"Yes, it's me. I'm surprised you realized it given my most excellent disguise." Lucifer flicked his hair. "My wife is feeling poorly, and so I am taking her place with the children."

"How traumatizing," was his candid reply.

The Devil's lips twitched. "That was the whole point. Aren't you in a fine mess."

"They're saying I killed someone." Dwayne grabbed the almost threadbare towel hanging on a hook and dried himself, ignoring the fact the Devil watched.

"Did you?"

He shrugged. "I don't remember, but I assume I must have since you're here to take me to Hell."

"Do I look like a taxi service to you?"

The rebuke had him stiffening. "Then why are you here?"

"The question is, why are you? What happened to being discreet?" the Devil demanded. "You know the angels are watching our operation. Winning that wager with them to keep it open doesn't mean you can go around killing people willy-nilly and getting caught. Why the fuck didn't you leave before the cops showed up?"

"I was trying not to draw attention. The humans would have noticed if I'd disappeared under their noses."

"They would have made an excuse. They're good at explaining away shit they don't understand." The Devil waved a hand. "But now they've got you on file and know you work for Grim Dating. You didn't just get caught, you fucked over my company. And to think I had such faith in your guild."

"Commander Brody and the other reapers had nothing to do with my error, Dark Lord. The blame is mine. I accept that I'm going to be sent back to Hell as punishment."

"Why would you go back there?" The Devil's nose wrinkled.

"Because I've been arrested."

"Which means your next task is to prove your innocence!" Lucifer declared with wave of an arm, which sent one of his silicone boobs sliding out the armpit of his dress.

"I'm being set up. No way they set me free." He hadn't forgotten the so-called evidence. "We'll need to coordinate an extraction effort."

Lucifer snorted. "Assist you in a prison breakout? Does this look like the Wild West? And why would you need help? We both know you can pop out anytime you want."

"Uh, no, I can't. My robe isn't working."

"What?" The Devil eyed him and frowned. "Since when?"

"Since I lost my memories last night."

"How unexpected." Lucifer rubbed his chin. "But I haven't time to deal with it now."

Dwayne grumbled, "I can't serve you if I'm sitting in a jail cell."

"Don't be so sure of that. I am quite fond of jailhouse musicals, and there's always someone to shank in prison. However, in your case, I need you out and about so you can do your work."

"Does this mean you're putting me back to reaping?" He brightened at the thought.

"No. I have more important things for you to do that require you remain on Earth for a while longer."

"You still want me to find the vampire, Noel?" Dwayne asked.

"Forget Noel. I'm surprised you haven't figured out the new task. The way I see it, someone has gone to great trouble here framing you. Covering their tracks with magic."

"Magic?"

Lucifer waved to the bag of clothes. "Any trace of who this blood belonged to has been wiped. No rewind. No sudden insights or visions."

"If someone died, though, you'd have gotten their soul."

"Would I?" Lucifer asked. "Numbers are down, and I thought to myself, maybe it's just that time of the century. No decent wars. Or plagues. But then I realized the population was higher than it's ever been. People had to be dying, I'm just not being notified about them." The Dark Lord's visage took on an ominous cast. "Someone is stealing my damned."

"How?" And who would dare target the king of Hell?

"If I knew how, they wouldn't be stealing them. Don't worry your rugged little head about it. I've got people working on that problem."

"Then what do you need me for?"

"Discover who is trying to bring down my company by framing you."

53

"What makes you think this was about Grim and not me?"

"Why would anyone target you? The only answer is no one would, meaning your arrest is merely a biproduct of an adversary aiming at me. Which makes no sense because all they did was draw attention to the weirdness of the situation. Unless," the Devil said, holding up his finger, "they want me distracted while they plot something even more devious."

"You think this frame job might be part of a larger plot."

Smoke drifted lazily from the Devil's nostrils. "Much bigger than you can imagine. Which is why you shall play along."

"Play along how?" He couldn't help a note of suspicion.

"Play along how, Dark Lord," Lucifer reminded.

"How are we playing along, Dark Lord?" he said through gritted teeth.

"Not me, you. You shall be a model prisoner."

"I'm not letting anyone bend me over," he snapped.

"Let's amend that to just don't let the humans see what you are and try not to cause too much damage or you'll make this more difficult than it already is."

"Not my fault I'm surrounded by idiots," Dwayne muttered as he gazed down at the snoring guard.

"He really is a moron. Not entirely his fault. His

parents were none too bright either. His brother, though, a fine minion. Different father you see," the Dark Lord explained.

"How long am I going to be rotting in a cell?"

"That all depends on the judge. But the good news is, I found you a lawyer."

"Cool. Experienced?"

"Yes. Excellent in their field. Reviled by the DA's office. You couldn't ask for a better champion in your corner."

"When can they spring me?"

"That depends on you. Right now, it's all circumstantial, especially since they don't have a body or a victim. Keep your nose clean and maybe you'll get out on bail."

"Maybe?" Dwayne finished tugging on the prison outfit, the fabric just as rough as expected. He was going soft.

The Devil smiled as Dwayne finally faced him again. "Humans are funny creatures. I can't always predict what they'll do. I mean look at the moron they elected in Canada," the Devil tossed over his shoulder as he bent over the cops, positioning their limbs.

"Don't you mean the United States?"

"It would be easier to name a country that doesn't have an idiot in charge. The point is, logically you should be released on bail. But I hate to give hope, so I'll temper it with reality. Luck is on her period, so you might get bitch-slapped and forced to remain in the clinker. If that happens, then we'll reevaluate."

"Fine."

"Fine what?" the Devil said, holding a hand to his ear.

"Fine, Dark Lord," Dwayne muttered as the Devil waggled his fingers and popped out of sight just as the cops roused, discovered themselves in a compromising state, and got into a shoving contest.

They got to their feet and looked around suspiciously. "What happened?"

"You told me if I watched you'd cut off my dick, so I showered while you and your partner had a moment." Dwayne arched a brow.

Taser cop shook his head and then turned to hiss at Ricky, "I told you not to touch me in public. What if my wife finds out?"

Ricky gaped. "I didn't—"

"Shut him the fuck up and let's get him to his cell."

"Yeah, Ricky. Come over here with your little dick and try and make me stay quiet."

"Mouthy fucker," Ricky huffed. "I know who to put you with. Hope you like spreading those cheeks dry." Ricky prodded him with a baton, jabbing him harder than needed.

He took stock of doors, possible exits, and cameras on his way to his cell. As cells went, it was almost as luxurious as his apartment. The mattress sank under his weight. The blanket was softer than his thick wool one. The air was much warmer too. He was less enthralled by the fucker on the top bunk, who thought he could leer, grab his crotch, and suggest what Dwayne could do with his mouth.

His cloak might not be working, but his fist could hit just fine.

It cracked across his roommate's jaw hard enough the man cried and got taken away. They only tried to stick him with one more detainee, who quickly screamed and begged to be moved, before they decided solitary was a better punishment.

He finally got some peace and quiet and some food. A tray of packaged dishes: sandwich, apple, gelatin, and apple juice.

Late afternoon, he was finally brought out of his cell and when he asked, "Where are we going?" the cop replied, "Your lawyer is here to see you."

"About fucking time," he muttered. Given he'd spoken to the commander the day before, he'd expected to be handled well before this.

They led him into a bland room, painted in a light gray, the walls pockmarked and scuffed. The metal table was bolted to the floor, as were the chairs.

The cuffs remained on his wrists, and he was tethered to the table. Nice to know they feared him. Although it probably didn't help his case.

The door slammed shut, and he sat waiting. Bored. Noticed the camera in the corner of the ceiling. The mirror across from him. A subtle scratch of his nose with his middle finger was probably caught by whoever watched.

When the door swung open, a petite woman entered, wearing a no-nonsense dark suit, her hair pulled back. She carried a briefcase and no coffee. What a shitty assistant. He looked beyond her, waiting for her boss.

When the door closed, he eyed her and said, "Where's my lawyer?"

"I'm your lawyer."

He eyed her up and down. He'd known his fair share of warriors, many of them female. But this woman…this human… She barely looked old enough to have gone to school, let alone have the experience to defend him.

"Yeah, you're not going to work," Dwayne drawled.

"Why not?"

"Too many reasons to count."

Her lips pressed tight. "I see. Would this have to do with the fact I pee sitting down?"

He almost smirked at her statement. "Partially." What he couldn't say was she was ill-suited mainly because of her humanity. The cops had obviously gotten tired of waiting for his real lawyer and sent him someone from the bullpen. "I don't need some overworked public defender. My company is springing for someone."

"Your company sent me," was her pert reply.

Again, he eyed her and then shook his head. "Bullshit."

"I assure you, Mr. Johnston, I am not kidding. Mr. Reaper himself hired me to handle your case, a trial run of sorts for a full-time position with your company."

"The commander sent you?" he blurted out before realizing he'd slipped.

"He did." She didn't remark on it.

He shook his head. "I don't believe you."

"I don't care about what you believe. I'm what you get. So stop being a prissy diva about it and handle it."

A scowl pulled his features. "You can't speak to me like that."

"I'll speak to you any damned way I please." She lifted her chin.

Could he be wrong about her? Perhaps she knew about Hell and the reapers. It was rare, but some humans got to share in their secret. "What if I say Lucifer?"

"I'd say if you're going to use being possessed as your defense, then you should know that it only rarely works and, at best, lands you in a mental institution taking a cocktail of drugs."

Either she was an excellent actress, or she didn't

know what he was and who he really worked for. Why would Brody have sent her? It had to be a mistake. "Tell the commander I want someone else."

"Tell him yourself. We're done here." She stood and gathered the folder she'd pulled from her briefcase.

He felt a twinge of guilt. She thought he'd fired her but for the wrong reason. "Sorry, but you're not ready to handle me. Maybe the commander will give you another shot with something else."

She uttered a sound of amusement. "You're assuming I'm quitting. Which I'm not. I was hired to defend your ungrateful ass, and that is what I intend to do, with or without your help." She stared at him, not flinching when he returned it.

"Are you hard of hearing? I don't want you as my lawyer."

"Oh, I hear you quite clearly. And I still don't care. So until you're willing to be reasonable, I guess you'll be spending more time than necessary in jail."

With that, she left, and he was returned to his cell.

Two days later, he was ready for her return, and when he was seated across from her snarled, "You win. What do you want me to do?"

5

Kourtney sat across from her client, who sported a few days' growth along his jaw. His expression remained as unbending and stern as before. His eyes the most dazzling shade of blue. His annoyance was clear in the tautness of his posture.

She sat down across from him. "Glad to see you've finally come to your senses."

"Don't gloat that I gave into your blackmail." A dark mutter.

"Don't be so difficult next time and I won't have to, Mr. Johnston." She pulled out his file, a slim one with nothing incriminating should anyone catch sight of it. She didn't need any information written down. She had a head for details, but it looked odd if she arrived empty-handed. Clients expected it too.

"What do you want me to do?"

"Make an attempt to look less like a thug for

court." She cocked her head. "Is that what you're wearing?"

He glanced down. "Don't like my very used, ill-fitting prison outfit? It's all the latest rage."

"Did no one bring you the suit I had sent ahead?"

"I doubt any suit you got your hands on would fit." He didn't have a frame that accommodated off-the-rack clothing.

"Are you saying the clothes in your closet don't belong to you?"

"My closet?" His fists clenched on the table. "You were in my apartment."

"I was. Not much to see. A shame we didn't get to it before the police did and took pictures. We could have fixed it first."

"My place is immaculate."

"Exactly. Totally unnatural." She shuddered. "We'll have to make it seem like you didn't move in long ago and haven't had time to fill it with crap and make it look lived in. Which then will raise the question of why you don't own anything at your age." She paused for a moment to eye him. "Did you lose your things in a fire?"

"No."

"Do you have a locker somewhere with personal items inside?"

"No."

"Someone else's items?"

His brows drew together as he growled. "No. I am new to this pla—" he stuttered, "place."

"Why were you in that club?" She changed the direction of questioning suddenly to catch him off guard.

"Why does it matter why I was there? I didn't kill anyone!" He sounded sure.

"Lucky for you, there is no body yet to say that you did. However, we need to act as if there is and counter it. It starts with a suit." She stood and strode to the door, banging on it until an officer opened it.

It was the young officer, Ricky something or other. "You done already?"

"I want Mr. Johnston's suit."

"He can't have anything that can be used as a weapon."

"I highly doubt the crease on his slacks is danger-ous," she retorted. "Now get that suit or I'll be telling the media how your incompetence has placed an innocent man behind bars and then denied him his basic rights."

"I'll see if I can locate it," Ricky mumbled.

The door shut, and she faced her client again. An impressive guy who might be part giant. He was big, but not fat. Wide and tall enough she could have climbed him. With all that muscle, he might not notice.

He looked mean enough to have killed someone. She'd yet to see any hint of softness in him, which was why she didn't allow any to seep past her expressions or words. She already knew he wouldn't respect anyone he perceived as weak, which was why she had played hardball with him and walked out.

The fact he'd only taken until late morning to send word he'd like to talk meant he wasn't completely irredeemable. So long as from here on in, he didn't do anything stupid, like whine about her doing her job, for example.

"You shouldn't have gone into my apartment."

"Are you still sulking about that? I had permission."

"Not from me," he grumbled.

"Building owner smelled smoke while I was talking to him. We, of course, had to go inside to check things out. It only made sense while I was there to grab you something to wear to court." It made her wonder what he was trying to hide. The place appeared ready to rent with hardly any furniture and no personal effects in sight.

There was no dresser in the bedroom, just a closet with a few hanging items. The suit being the biggest surprise. Then again, Mr. Johnston had been in trouble before. Having met him, she was sure it happened more often than perhaps documented.

He drummed his fingers, angrily. Guiltily? Perhaps he feared she'd find something. Had he hidden a body under his floor? In the wall? Perhaps he'd stashed mementos from his victims.

"You do realize, I work for you, Mr. Johnston. Not the DA's office. Not even Grim Dating. My task is to free you."

"A suit ain't going to make anyone believe I'm innocent."

"But wearing that will?" She flicked her hand in his direction, indicating the worn prison outfit.

"Don't get me wrong, I'll wear the suit. But it won't wash me of the blood they found me covered with."

"Ah yes, the fluid covering you and the crime scene. I'm glad you mentioned it." She pulled out a sheet of paper, the logo of a lab at the top and the rest scrawled with graphs and numbers. The results of the quick forensics done on the samples. "Lucky for you, they're not sure what kind of blood that is. Or if it even is blood."

"Not blood?" He straightened in his seat. "If that's the case, then there's no crime. I can be freed."

She pursed her lips. "If only if were that simple. "

"It is that simple. No blood. No body. At best, they'll charge me with breaking and entering after the club closed. Possibly mischief."

"Except, the DA has a victim. A patron of the club. She's now been missing for more than forty-eight hours. Her purse was found on the scene."

"And? Doesn't make her dead," he blurted out.

"No, but you are a person of interest, as not only is there is a witness claiming you were seen with her but they found a necklace she owned in your apartment."

He stared at her before exclaiming, "That's bull-shit. I'm being framed."

"I agree that someone is really keen on having you charged and isn't afraid to bend the rules."

The door opened without warning, and Ricky thrust a hanger strung with plastic into the room. "Found it. But you only got four minutes before the van comes to get him."

"Thank you."

The cop waited.

"Was there something you need? You are wasting those four minutes."

"Aren't you gonna leave?" asked Ricky.

She smirked. "I'm not done talking to my client. So out. Now. Shoo." She waved her hand, and Ricky left.

Her client drawled, "That should get spit in my dinner later."

"You won't be in here for dinner, or breakfast. We are walking out of that courthouse today."

"What happened to this isn't going to be simple?"

She snapped her briefcase shut. "I thrive when challenged."

"Great, I'm a game for you," he said, rustling some plastic.

"Would it help if I said I like to win?" She resisted the urge to turn around. Why bother when, from the corner of her eye, the mirrored window showed him stripped to change.

That was a lot of skin. A lot of muscle. She found herself swallowing at the sight of the fur on his chest, stroking down his body, arrowing through the vee to the waistband of his pants. He pulled them down, and she quickly averted her gaze.

Still heard a low chuckle.

Her cheeks heated as she realized he'd caught her watching. Unethical. And her silence even worse. She was wasting time. "When we get out there, I want you to plead not guilty."

"Because you think I'm dumb enough to admit I committed an imaginary crime." He snorted as he crossed his arms, straining the linen of his shirt.

"Well, you were caught covered in a suspicious substance, claiming ignorance as to how you got there."

"Should have known you'd use logic."

She arched a brow. "Appalling, isn't it? That women can think and reason better than a man." She'd met sexists in her life, but he was something else in his disdain.

"Lose the chip. I don't care what's between your legs."

"I wouldn't say that in public in case word gets

back to the judge. She's recently divorced and man hating, according to rumor."

"In other words, smile, lie, and play nice. May the Dark Lord see my evil deeds." He lowered his gaze and then shook his head.

"And that's another thing. No weird sarcasm or references to the Devil. You're going to try and appear like a law-abiding citizen who was taken advantage of in a club and the victim of a horrible prank and robbery."

"The police have my phone and wallet."

"But no credit or bank cards."

"Don't have any."

"Your keys were missing."

"Don't have those either."

The reply stumped her for a second. "How can you not have a key? Your apartment was locked. Don't tell me you scale the outside wall and go in a window?"

"There is a fire escape."

"That probably hasn't seen any use in at least a decade."

He flattened his lips. "I keep a spare close by."

"And do you hide money inside your prison wallet in case you need it too?" she asked, grabbing his file and stuffing it into her case.

"I had cash in my pocket."

"It didn't appear on the report."

"You think the cops took it?"

"They aren't going to admit it, which means we can use robbery as a probable cause."

Bang. Bang. "Time's up," Ricky shouted from the hall.

"Dammit. Are you ready?"

"Doesn't matter if I am or not, does it?"

At least he understood. "Let's get you out of here."

6

EVEN DWAYNE COULDN'T DENY the fact his bail hearing wasn't going well.

The prosecution's office played to the audience, the curiosity seeking filling the seats. They wouldn't actually decide the case; that would depend on the judge. She'd rule whether or not this case had enough evidence to go to trial and, if yes, whether he'd be returning to his cell or released on bail. Given her expression, he was wagering on the latter.

The prosecutor, a tall man with an impressive midsection, paced back and forth as he argued, twisting even the most banal thing into a sure sign of Dwayne's guilt.

How was the fact he had no condiments in his fridge a crime? Cooking wasn't a skill he'd ever had to learn. In Hell, there were no reliable fridges. No kitchens in the tiny rooms they were assigned while living in the guild. Only married couples ever moved out.

Most reapers were single. And they didn't cook.

He frowned as the prosecutor then launched into a rant, making the fact he used a single soap to wash his skin and hair sound like another kind of crime.

Clean was clean.

Eventually, the list of all the things he might have done wrong came to an end, and the audience clapped. It took effort not to yawn and stretch as if he'd just woken.

Slapping her hands on the table, his lawyer stood, startling the applause. It petered out as she said, "You should have been a fantasy writer because that was quite the story. Were you planning to put any facts in there at all?" The delivery was beautiful.

The prosecutor gaped. "There's a preponderance of evidence."

"Of circumstance, which I'm going to prove isn't a crime." And then his lawyer with the tiny frame, but massive presence, offered her rebuttal.

Just as overblown as the prosecution's, but it made some strong points such as the fact they still didn't have a body. A filed missing person report didn't automatically make it a murder. And then the piece de resistance. She waved the lab results for the blood that had covered his clothes and body. "Ladies and gentlemen"—she gave it a shake—"no matter how it might have appeared, the substance covering

Mr. Johnston remains unidentified." She put the sheet down and then took a moment to let her gaze track around the room and end on the judge. "They don't know what it is. So exactly where is this murder they're talking of? If there's no blood, and no body, then what's left?"

It was a masterful finish.

The crowd took a moment to let it sink in. They didn't need to clap. It was so obvious he had done nothing wrong.

The prosecutor jumped in and claimed it was blood, and that the false reading was because of contamination. Apparently, a lab was working on the problem, whereupon his lawyer subtly hinted they were doctoring results.

That led to some shouting and being called in front of the judge. They went into the judge's chambers, leaving him to sit at his table, bored by the proceeding but more and more intrigued by Ms. Kourtney Blake.

She didn't care if he was a killer. She had one goal and one only: Defend him to the best of her abilities. Convincingly too. Impressive given she didn't like him.

He'd yet to correct her misconceptions. She probably still wrongly assumed his desire to remove her from his case had to do her sex when really what bothered him most was her humanity. She only knew a portion of the story. Didn't have access to all the information.

How could she truly defend or even help him discover who was behind the framing?

He needed someone else.

Soon.

Real soon, as the sight of her emerging from chambers looking annoyed caused his cape to ripple for the first time since that night. Why did it react to her? He hoped it wasn't a precursor because it sensed she was marked for death.

He preferred to think the reaction of his cloak was just a coincidence. His magic finally wakened. When it did…he wouldn't have to stay anywhere he didn't want.

His lawyer sat with hard thump by his side and began to scribble.

"What's wrong?" he whispered.

"The judge is being a hardass. It would have helped if you didn't look like a serial killer in the front row. Sit up straight. Try and not look like you're thinking of ways to murder everyone in the room."

"But I am." He smirked.

That brought a frown. "Don't smile. And stop staring at me. People have noticed, and it just increases your creep factor."

He stilled his drumming fingers. "I am not staring at you."

The arrival of the judge called them to attention, and court resumed.

Kourtney was still frowning, her lips pinched.

Angry.

Sexy.

She glanced at him then wrote something on a pad.

Eyes in front.

She'd caught him. Shameful. Why couldn't he keep his eyes off her?

He glanced forward just as the judge swung her glasses his way. She caught his gaze.

He smiled. At least attempted to. Heard his lawyer mutter, "You idiot."

The judge grimaced. "I think I've heard enough. It is my belief there is ample evidence to go forward with this case."

"What case? There's no body," his lawyer argued.

"No, but we do have a missing young lady and your client at the center of it all."

"Most of the evidence is circumstantial at best."

"If that's true, then you'll have no issue convincing a jury of his innocence. But I doubt it." The judge's lip curled. "Anyone can see there's a darkness around him."

The strange remark cocked his head. Could the judge see the shadow of his cloak? That probably meant she didn't have long left.

"Are you calling Mr. Johnston evil?" His legal counsel made it sound mocking.

The judge didn't back down. "I'm saying there is something off about him."

"Your opinion is irrelevant," his lawyer snapped. He could have told her not to bother. For whatever reason, the judge appeared predisposed to dislike him.

"Please. As if you haven't noticed it yourself. I've seen the report detailing how clean and empty his apartment is. Living there over three months and yet his cupboards are bare. He's got almost no furniture."

"I don't like clutter," he muttered, earning himself a kick from his lawyer.

She clasped her hands. "Your honor, tidiness is not a crime."

"No, it's not, but he's not being charged with being too clean but for the murder of Ms. Lakely."

"How can you even claim it's murder when the substance recovered at the scene was fake blood?" How hotly his legal counsel defended him.

The prosecution finally interjected. "It is our belief the initial testing was contaminated."

"Does this mean you're going to try and shop the fluid around until you find someone who will tell you what you want to make a case?" his lawyer accused.

"I'm sure everyone will maintain professional

integrity. And I will add, we wouldn't be having this conversation at all if Mr. Johnston could explain how he came to be in that club, in the possession of an item belonging to our missing lady, covered in a blood-like substance."

"As you're well aware, he was dosed with a drug that has compromised his memories."

"Seems rather convenient."

"Are you going to victim blame?" his tiny dynamo argued. "What happened to innocent until proven guilty?"

She might have gone a tad too far. The courtroom hushed as they waited for the judge's reply.

Leaning forward, her face serious, the judge said, "Since you're so convinced he isn't a threat to society, then does that mean you are willing to take responsibility for his actions?"

"I will gladly post his bond."

"I'm talking about more than money. I'm talking about making you personally accountable for your client by having him be your constant companion until we discover the truth."

"Excuse me?"

His lawyer wasn't the only one who didn't grasp what that meant. "Say what?" He straightened in his seat.

"It is my decision that, pending more test results and the location of the missing Ms. Lakely, the bail be set at one hundred thousand dollars contingent on Mr. Johnston being kept within visual distance of Ms. Blake at all times."

"You can't make me his jailor," she squeaked.

The judge smirked, and for just a moment, he saw a glint in her eyes, a spark that told him something otherworldly was at play here, influencing her decision. "Jail is for criminals. A client staying with you is a guest thing. Unless you are saying he *is* a criminal, in which case we could leave him in jail."

His lawyer simmered. "This is highly unorthodox."

"What can I say? I like to think outside of the box," the judge said a little too sweetly. "We'll reconvene to see where this case is at in a week."

"A week!" Kourtney squeaked. "You can't do this."

The gavel slammed. "I just did."

"I protest."

"Don't make me hold you in contempt, Kourtney."

"Listen, Marybel—"

"It's Judge Peters. And I'm serious. Keep talking and I'll have you fined." The gavel lifted.

"No need," she huffed. "I have no problem at all with Mr. Johnston staying in my home as a guest."

"Then it's settled." The judge swept out of the courtroom.

"Fucking bitch." He would have sworn her lips never moved, but he heard it nonetheless.

Of more interest to him was the conversation at the end. "You know the judge by first name?"

"We went to school together," she muttered. "Not a big deal."

"Apparently it was because that woman hates you." The smug satisfaction had given it away.

"It was years ago. While we were in college."

"And she's still pissed?"

"Some people know how to hold a grudge."

"What did you do?"

A debate raged in her eyes as she decided whether or not to tell him. She sighed. "Not my fault her professor was being sexually inappropriate. He got suspended, and the students he was sleeping with didn't get a grade for that class, meaning she was missing a credit needed to maintain a scholarship. When it fell through, she almost dropped out."

"You were the one to report the indiscretion that you might take the scholarship from her." The evilness of it had an elegance.

"And if I did?" She shrugged as she tucked her papers together to put them in her briefcase. "She deserved to be disqualified in favor of someone legitimate. She was cheating to get a better grade."

"You've never cheated?"

"I've never been caught," was her reply. She finished clearing her space, doing a spectacular job of ignoring the questions being shouted at them by the media at the back of the room.

He had no problem tuning them out. Humans didn't have anything to say that he needed to hear. Except for the one standing beside him.

"You'll have to give me a few minutes to arrange the bail."

He frowned. "I thought the judge gave me permission to leave."

"Once the bail is handled, which means a bit of paperwork. It shouldn't be too long."

Apparently, the judge meant what she said. He had to remain within close proximity of his lawyer. To ensure compliance, they both wore ankle bracelets set to a frequency that would scream and alert a central office if they got too far apart.

They got their first example as they went to leave the station. He strode ahead, and the moment the door swung shut behind him, the anklet began to chirp louder and louder, only choking off when his lawyer joined him outside.

She glanced down at their ankles then muttered, "This is insane. They shouldn't be this sensitive."

"Haven't you figured out yet that nothing about my case is normal?" He could almost taste the magic at work.

That earned him a glare. "Come back inside and give me a second while I go yell at someone."

It wouldn't matter how much she argued. Whatever force had him arrested, and paired with this angry human, obviously wasn't done yet.

The alarm went off the moment she went into an office. Sitting in a chair, Dwayne tilted his head back and had a nap.

Not a very good one with all the whispering. When his lawyer returned, she still wore the ankle bracelet and an annoyed expression as she marched past, barking, "Let's go."

A good thing he had a long stride because she walked quickly and with purpose, her smaller stature not needing long legs, given she took two to his one.

"I take it you didn't win that last round."

Her gaze slewed in his direction. "Don't talk. Not here." She marched with even more purpose, and he let himself be swept along in her wake.

The sun felt nice after a few days in artificial lighting. He angled his face into it, earning him a terse, "Stop giving them photo ops. Let's go."

Only then did he notice the curiosity seekers with their phones. A few even had actual cameras.

He scowled and wished for the concealment of his robe. He hated being corporeal all the time. It made him too visible when he just wanted to be forgotten.

His lawyer snapped her fingers and drew some of the watchers. "If you must have a statement, it is simply that Mr. Johnston is not guilty and this is a travesty of justice."

"Does he know Ms. Lakely?"

"No."

"Whose blood was it?" someone else asked.

"Didn't you hear? It wasn't blood at all," she declared as a sleek black car slid to the curb. The driver popped out, quickly opening the rear passenger door.

She slid in, but he didn't immediately follow, which was why he heard the last question. More like a ribald suggestion. "Given the judge's restrictions, will you be sleeping together?"

To his annoyance, his body was more than ready to say yes.

7

DWAYNE SCOWLED as he joined Kourtney in the car. The door closed, making her aware of the small space between them and the privacy from eyes, given the front seat was sectioned off. The Town Car service Grim Dating provided proved to be a nice luxury.

A good thing the job had some perks, given Mr. Johnston ignored her. Asshole. And after she'd had him set free on bail. Albeit with conditions. Still, why did he have to appear so annoyed? Was spending time with her that onerous?

"I can't believe she'd stoop to such a petty revenge," she huffed, holding out her foot to glare at the electronic tracker circling her ankle.

"Don't pretend to be the victim here. This is entirely your fault," he pointed out. "You knew she hated you and yet still chose to go in front of her."

"The incident happened over a decade ago. It obviously didn't hold her back. Tempered steel and all that." It sounded weak even to her ears. Still, if she had to do it again... She regretted nothing.

"You of all people should know everyone likes holding on to a grudge. It's the level of revenge that differs," was his wise and unhelpful offering.

"We're professionals."

"No, you're not," he emphasized. "You've already admitted you'll do pretty much anything to defend a client."

"Not true. I would never kill anyone."

"Unless you could claim self-defense."

"Obviously. I am not about to allow anyone to kill me."

He shook his head. "I can see why you might have come to the attention of the guild. Tell me, was it the Dark Lord himself who referred you to the commander?"

She blinked. "That was a whole lot of crazy. We are going to have to coach you on the right and wrong things to say."

He pursed his lips. "There is nothing amiss with my words."

"Which is the first problem. You can't tell me a moderately intelligent fellow like yourself can't see it."

"Never claimed to be smart. Just speaking the truth."

"Your version of the truth sounds like the crazy voice that is supposed to stay inside your head. You sound insane, which, in turn, makes you appear guilty. Are you doing this on purpose to make my job harder? Is this part of your company's test?"

"If you can't handle it..." He shrugged as the words trailed off.

"You'd like that, wouldn't you?" she huffed. "I'm not quitting."

"Good for you. There's the spirit." Totally meant to annoy her. He leaned forward to rap on the window.

"What are you doing?"

"Giving the driver a location to drop me."

The privacy window slid open. "Can I help?"

Dwayne leaned even closer. "Hey, Bert. Can you take me to my place?"

She threw herself forward. "Ignore that order, Bert. Proceed as discussed." She hit the button and closed the partition.

"As discussed?" He arched a brow. "Why, Kourtney, are you kidnapping me?"

"That's Ms. Blake."

"I like Kourtney better," he needled. "Where you are taking me, Counselor? Weekend getaway for two? Cement factory for some concrete shoes?"

"Those are kind of opposite extremes."

"I'd say my option in either direction is fifty-fifty."

"Well, they're both wrong," she stated. "We're going home."

"Why didn't you say so? Can't wait to sleep in my bed."

Was he being intentionally clueless? "You can't go back to your apartment."

"Why the fuck not?"

Her lips pursed. "For one, you know the conditions of your bail. You stay with me. And second, your apartment is a crime scene."

"Nothing happened there."

"Says you. The detective on your case thinks you knew you were going to be caught and recently cleaned the place. He's putting in demands to have a more thorough inspection done."

"That's ridiculous," he growled. "I did nothing wrong. I'm being framed."

"Obviously." She could see the reply took him aback.

"You believe me?" he asked almost cautiously.

Her slim shoulders rolled. "A man like you wouldn't be sloppy if he killed someone. You're too impatient for stupidity. The reports also claim you looked high when you were found, but tox screens taken at the scene didn't show any of the usual suspects."

"Someone took my blood? I don't remember any needles."

"Urine sample. Apparently, you actually agreed to pee in a cup."

"I vaguely recall that." His brow wrinkled. "I was still fucked up when they asked me."

"Which is why we might be able to have the urine tossed out if it turns out to not help us."

"How could my piss help?" he exclaimed, somewhat angrily.

"Because if you were drugged, then we can claim you weren't yourself. Or incapable of the accusation. Urine, though, doesn't give us the best picture. I wish they'd conned you into giving blood."

"You need my blood?" He held out his arm.

"Yes, but not right this second. I don't have the right tools, and I wouldn't put much hope in it. Whatever you had in your system has probably flushed by now, meaning we need to look at other scenarios to shift the blame. Such as who would want to have you arrested."

"Nobody that's still living hates me."

"And how did all those people die?" Was she trying to defend a psychopath? She eyed the partition. Had she made a mistake enclosing herself with him?

He softly chuckled. "Wasn't me that killed them. Most died of old age."

"And those that didn't?"

"The Devil sent a reaper to claim their souls." He feigned a smile. It did nothing to soften the claim.

"You need to work on your humor. It is much too dry."

"I'm not a comedian."

"Never said you were funny, but you do have your Wednesday Addams persona almost down pat."

"Who?"

"You don't know Wednesday Addams? Hold on. Let me find some pictures." The internet had plenty to show, and he didn't even blink as she scrolled through a few on her phone.

He blinked. "You compared me to a little girl."

"This is less about gender than the goth personality you're displaying with a willful refusal to act normal."

"I am normal. This is who I am."

That drew a snort. "Would you stop with the bullshitting? Because I don't believe it for a second. I understand you probably have this persona you have to exude because of your job. I get it. Grim Dating. You gotta pretend you're morbid and dour. Make vague references to the taking of souls and stuff as if you're the bringer of death."

"I am a reaper."

"Let me guess, reaper is your company's cute name for matchmaker. Kudos to the marketing department. It's catchy, if weird, but then again, there are lots of weird people in the world, so I can see how it would appeal."

He stared at her. "You really don't know anything at all, do you?"

"I know that you're good at playing charades, but now the game has to stop."

"It is because of disbelievers like you that it so easy to work right under your noses. Humanity can be so blind to the truth."

"What have I said about talking crazy?"

"Why me, Dark Lord," he muttered.

"Don't make me get you a gag so you can practice keeping your mouth shut."

He glared at her. Let him. She had other things to do, such as check her junk mail.

He wouldn't be ignored. "I don't care if my pad is fucked up. That's where I want to go. Hell, drop me off at one of my buddy's if you have to."

"What part of the ankle bracelets need to be in close range do you not understand?" she snapped.

"Don't tell me you didn't get them to expand the distance."

"The only exception I managed was a half-hour for bathroom breaks once a day so we can shower with privacy."

"Only a half-hour? That's not enough time." He grunted.

No, it wasn't, but hopefully it wouldn't be for more than a night. She was going in front of a different judge in the morning regarding these strange bail conditions.

"How do I know your home is up to my standards?"

She gaped at him. "Given your standards were a cheap recliner and a mattress, I'd say you'll be fine."

"I have no need of luxury."

"Maybe you didn't need it, but having it would have made you seem more normal. They would have been able to relate to you."

"Fuck that. I ain't got nothing in common with humans." He actually shuddered.

"Once again, I will reiterate that it is that odd humor that will make the case more difficult. We have lots of work to do to prove your innocence."

"So you now believe me when I say I didn't do it?"

"What I think doesn't matter. It's all about what I can convince a jury of if this goes to trial."

"I thought you were supposed to get the case tossed?" he accused.

"That's still my first plan. But in case it doesn't work, I need to be thinking ahead. Meaning you and I will have to sit down and go over what happened that night. I'm still fuzzy on some of the facts."

"Because I don't remember anything."

"Which is something we'll work on. Could be you'll remember something we can use."

"Remember or fabricate?"

She looked him dead in the eye as she said, "Mr. Johnston, I would never ask you to lie."

8

DWAYNE MIGHT HAVE BELIEVED Kourtney if he hadn't heard another voice—also hers— say, *Is he really that stupid? As if I'd ever say anything like that out loud.*

He stared at her, but she ignored him, head bent. Had she spoken? He drew away from her to huddle against the car's door, his cloak momentarily flowing over his upper body, a short respite before it fell lifeless again. "I would prefer we get the charges dropped before it goes to trial."

"Then work with me, not against me."

"I don't know if I can. Seems kind of counterintuitive to be cooperating with my jailor."

"Host." Her jaw gritted.

"And I am your guest for now, but given how close we must be to each other, perhaps more? After all, given the rules of our imprisonment, we'll have to share a bed. I should warn you I sleep in the nude

and usually wake up horny." He was being intentionally crude. He had to be so she could see how absurd
this was and do something to stop it. Stop it before
he kissed those lips. Would they remain hard and
demanding against his or soften, melting at his
touch?

His words should have thrown her off balance,
but instead, she smiled coolly. "Get ready to have
your fantasy crushed. One, I sleep fully clothed and
wake up bitchier than you'd believe. I also kick in my
sleep. Good news, though, there is a divan in my
room, so you'll have your own bed."

He glanced at his frame then tilted one corner of
his mouth. "I highly doubt I'll fit."

"Then there's always the floor."

"Only if you join me on it." He baited her again.

"For a man who wants me to set him free, you're
doing your best to turn me against you. Why?"

The pointed query had him suddenly regarding
his actions in a new light. Why did he fight her? She
seemed to know her shit. Had already gotten him
released, albeit under some strange conditions. Had
she known exactly who he was, he would have never
even argued.

On the other hand, she had her flaws. She
verbally sparred with him. Belittled him. Had no
respect or fear. In other words, had already proven
herself under adversity. Imagine what she could
accomplish if they allied.

He eyed her. "Guess I owe you an apology for being a dick."

"Lucky for you, your bosses are willing to pay lots if I win this thing. I could get used to this kind of perk." She ran her hand over the leather seat.

"Don't you have a car?" He saw her in something sleek, fully equipped. Leather seats that reclined, with her skirt pulled up...

"I do, but it's an old piece of shit. Despite my scholarships, I have student loans. A new car isn't on the horizon. Especially now that I'm looking for a full-time gig."

The revelation had him eyeing her in a new light. Tough because life had tempered her. She'd had to fight and save for the things she wanted. Something he could respect.

And that esteem only grew when he finally saw her house.

For some reason, he'd expected her to live some-where posh, polished, like her. Instead, their ride pulled into the driveway of a house that appeared elegant, if old. As in built at the last turn of the century.

The entire street was lined with homes that had seen better days. A few had tried to rejuvenate with paint. One had been replaced with something so modern it hurt the eyes.

The house that confronted him hadn't yet gotten the same kind of face lift, but he saw signs the restoration had begun. Wooden steps featured raw, unstained wood—probably to replace rotted sections. Railings and posts were scraped clean, ready for a fresh coat of paint.

Inside the front hall, black and white tile covered the floor and was reflected in a closet with mirrored doors. To the side of the hanging key rack was a flashing screen. She stood in front of it and let it scan her face. The light steadied as the alarm disarmed.

He couldn't help but remark, "Facial recognition won't save you if an intruder grabs you by the head and holds you in front of it."

"Tongue between my lips, two rapid blinks, or the twitch of my nose will launch the panic mode."

He glanced at the screen then her. "That already occurred to you."

"I deal with criminals. I know their tricks. I'm not falling for any of them."

Did the violence sometimes follow her home? How dare anyone try and harm her!

His cloak rippled and swelled, snapping past the boundaries of this world and the nebulous one it existed in.

But she saw nothing, as she'd already pivoted and padded inside the closest arch. His mantle stilled. He tried to get it to twitch, but it was as inanimate as the rest of his outfit.

Following his lawyer, Dwayne found himself in

what might have once been a living room but had since become an office. In here, the renovation was complete, with the floor shining, the walls perfectly plastered and painted, the wainscoting dent and scuff free. From the ceiling, a chandelier with dangling crystals hung.

The desk was an antique, massive enough he wondered how they got it in. He eyed the clawed ornate feet.

"They screw into the bottom. A good thing or it wouldn't have fit through the door."

"This is where you do business?" Her home didn't seem like a smart place to invite criminals.

"No. Usually I'm at the police station, jails, and court. Since I stopped working for the public defender's office, any other meetings with clients take place in coffee shops or restaurants."

"I'm public." He couldn't help but utter a soft chuckle. "I guess this makes me special."

"Don't make me regret it," she stated, moving around the desk. Putting it between them? Or was she really diving into her work?

He noticed the built-in shelves filled with rows of leather-bound tomes. When she said nothing, he asked, "Did I hear you say you worked for the public defender's office?"

"I did until a few months ago. Which is lucky for you. I've gone up against the DA enough times I know exactly how they do things over there. If it costs lots of money, you can bet they'll try and wiggle out of it. Meaning we will push for all kinds of tests and reports, which they'll deny, allowing us to claim they don't want to exonerate because they know their case is weak. Eventually they won't have a choice but to concede."

"You mean to wear them down."

"Hopefully it won't take too long," she absently replied as she rifled through a stack of papers.

"Or we could actually prove I'm innocent."

"Much harder to do and less likely to win."

The reply brought a frown. "How is it less likely?"

"They'll try and get anything we find that helps get it tossed out. And I know they're going to do this because that is exactly what I'm about to do with some of their evidence." She pulled something out of the pile and put it aside.

"What happened to justice being about the truth?"

She laughed, the sound a short, surprised bark. "Oh, you silly man. The truth is decided by the victors, and that is whoever weaves the most believable tale."

"I'd like to win by showing them they're wrong."

That caused her to pause and glance at him. "Are you sure you want us to dig for the truth? Right now, you have plausible deniability. You remember nothing. What if you do start to scratch at the crime and you discover you're not as guiltless as you hoped?"

"If I did anything, then I had a damned good reason."

Her head cocked. "The I-was-made-to-do-it defense. Not my favorite, but it might work if you can prove you were in mortal peril." She gestured for a seat across from her. "Sit down, and let's finally have a proper interview, Mr. Johnston. Tell me about yourself."

His mouth opened, and he almost told her. Almost told about her about the dumb fucking mechanic who started fixing bikes for a local gang on the side, making cash under the table. Good money, too, considering the tax man wasn't taking a cut. It wasn't long until he was fixing them full-time and hanging out with their owners at night.

Drugs. Women. Alcohol. Those years were a blur even now. He'd spent most of them fucked up. Bikers knew how to party. They also knew how to get into trouble.

The night he got caught in the crossfire came about as a result of a vendetta. Simply, Gang A pissed off Gang B. Gang B knew where to exact retribution: the garage where someone from Gang A would be picking up a bike. Never mind that the mechanic fixing it was just an ordinary guy.

Dwayne never forgot the thuds of bullets hitting his flesh. He died slowly, leaking on the floor, each breath a bubbling, painful mess. When he finally expired, seconds after the first responders arrived, off to Hell he went, but it took some prodding. The reaper assigned to him was forced to drag him with a silvery lasso.

At times, he wondered if he should have refused Lucifer's offer after he'd crossed the Styx. He did, after all, have a choice.

The Dark Lord, sitting high above on his podium of judgment, had leaned down with those flame-colored eyes and whispered, "What's it going to be, Dwayne, not-my-favorite-rock, Johnston? Are you going to become one of the mindless damned, eking out an existence in Hell? Or do you want purpose as one of my prized reapers?"

When put like that...

Being a reaper hadn't been all that bad. The guys in the guild were his brothers, and he liked the magical cloak.

A hunk of fabric that now hung uselessly down his back. Had the drug that wiped his memories killed it? Would it ever recover?

Caught in his own head, he suddenly realized Kourtney stared at him.

"What?" he barked.

"I asked you to give me a quick biography, and you just went somewhere else." She snapped her fingers. "I need you here. Answering my questions."

"I don't see what my past has to do with anything."

"Then you are dumber than I thought. Because I

can think of a few reasons already." She began to tick them off her fingers. "Ex-spouse or girlfriend. Jealous coworker. Family feud. A vendetta. Stalker."

"I thought stalkers took pictures and left creepy presents in beds," was his reply.

"Have you found any decapitated heads in your apartment? Mutilated body parts of animals?"

"No."

"Phone calls with breathing or hanging up? Mail gone missing or appearing as if it were opened? Things in your apartment seeming slightly off?"

"No one has been spying on me."

"Then what about one of the other possibilities?"

"No."

"Are you sure? You haven't really thought about it."

"No point when none of them fit. I have no past relationships that would care enough to even remember my name. Nor have I been living here long enough to form any attachments."

"Family? Friends?"

"Family is dead." Mostly. Once he was buried, it wasn't as if he had any reason to keep in touch. Given it had been over fifty years—he'd died in the '70s—most weren't around anymore and wouldn't remember the black sheep who got himself killed.

"You do have friends?" she asked, almost as if seeking reassurance.

"Yeah, and trust me when I say none of them would be fucking with me like this."

"Wishful thinking doesn't count. We'll need to check them out." She made some notes. "Let's talk about your day-to-day routine. What's it typically look like?"

"Not complicated. Go to work, go home."

"Surely you do more than that."

"I buy food on the way home. Mostly premade stuff from restaurants."

"Do you also purchase alcohol?"

"I don't drink." Hadn't since he died, although he did smoke the occasional joint.

"What about going to the movies? Bowling? Yoga?"

"I am not doing anything that has me crouching like a dog." He shook his head at each. "Work, food, home."

"Do you ride the subway?"

He hesitated before saying, "I walk."

"Everywhere?" She stared at him.

"I only go to work."

"That's quite a few miles."

"I keep fit." And it wasn't completely out of the realm of believability.

"The night of the incident, you went to that club."

"Yes." No point in denying it when she stated it as fact.

"It's on the other side of town."

He saw the trap. "I took a taxi that night."

"Receipt?"

"I paid cash." He lied, and she didn't call him on it, just took notes.

"Why did you go to the club?"

"Would you believe Lucifer sent me on a mission to find a missing vampire?" He gave her the dead-pan truth.

"Save that bullshit in case we need it for an insanity plea."

"Nothing wrong with my mental state," he complained. Why did he keep blurting out the truth? Did he want her to know what he really was?

"Tell me about the club. Why did you go there?"

"I was looking for a place to party. I walked by, heard the music, and thought I'd go inside to check it out."

"I thought you took a cab."

She'd caught him.

"I took the taxi to a restaurant, a pizza place with handmade dough. I had dinner before going for a walk. I heard the music, and intrigued by it, I decided to check it out."

She stopped taking notes, the tip of her pencil resting on the pad of paper. "Don't ever use that lie in court."

"What lie? The food? I can give you the name of a restaurant, but I doubt they'll remember me. They were busy that night."

"And let me guess, you paid cash. That's fine. That's believable. It's the rest of it. You are not the type to be lured by boom-boom music and frothy, overpriced booze."

"What type am I?"

"Fire pit, coffee, in the woods, by a lake."

His turn to make a disparaging noise. "Never done that once in my life." Never got to do a lot of things.

"Maybe you should. Might make you relax."

"I don't need to relax," was his sarcastic reply. "What I need is to remember what the fuck happened to me after I went inside."

"Did you drink anything?" She returned to business.

"No."

"Are you sure?"

"I had a beverage, but it was for show so I wouldn't be empty-handed while I scouted the place."

"Looking for a victim?"

"No!" A partial lie. He had been looking for someone.

She paused her writing again. "You might as well admit you were seeking a hookup; otherwise, it just makes you look creepy."

He hated she had a point. "Fine, I was looking for someone."

"Did you find them?"

"No. I don't think so." His brow furrowed as he tried to recall.

"What's the last thing you remember?"

Straining didn't help him pierce that blank spot in his mind. "I remember wondering how people actually enjoyed that place. The music was much too loud and annoying. The drink artificial crap. The club should have been paying people to drink, not overcharging them."

"So you got your glass and you're mingling."

"I don't mingle. I found a spot to watch."

"Watch who?"

At that point? "Everyone."

"When you spot a person of interest, then what?"

"I never got to that point. Watching is the last thing I recall before waking up to the cops shouting at me."

She tapped her lip with the pencil. "Whatever they doped you with caused some memory loss. I'll need to get your urine retested."

"You said I didn't have any indications of drugs."

"The usual ones. We're going to test it deeper. Along with your blood. Even though it's been awhile. If we're lucky, there might still be traces." She opened a drawer and pulled out a plastic case.

He pursed his lips as she flipped it open to show everything she needed to draw blood. "I hardly see how this would be admissible."

"Because we are videotaping it." She placed her

phone on a tripod on her desk. "Tell the camera your name and the date."

She coached him through it all and was verbose as she labelled the sample, sealed it, placed it into an envelope, and then hand addressed it. Only once she'd shown it being handed off to the FedEx guy did she finally stop filming.

"That seemed excessive."

"It's more than the cops ever do and will create doubt when it comes back laced with all kinds of stuff."

"And if it doesn't?"

She patted his cheek. "Don't worry. It will."

9

THE INTERVIEW DIDN'T ACCOMPLISH much, nor did it abate her awareness of him. On the contrary, it only heightened it.

When Kourtney had accused Dwayne of watching her, she'd almost gotten caught. A good thing he'd not grasped that in order for her to know, she had to be keeping a discreet eye on him.

Why did she keep staring? Sure, he was handsome, if scruffy. His hair a shaggy layer that she wanted to comb with her fingers. His jaw square, sporting a shadow. Handsome when he wasn't sneering. He'd be killer if he smiled.

And she was spending the night with him.

It was beyond absurd she had to have him in her house, and not just in her space but in her bedroom.

She shoved her hand into a bag of chips and guzzled a non-caffeine can of Coke. Horrible for her, but when she'd had a high-stress day, it did something to calm her. Relaxed her into wanting to sleep.

She had a college acquaintance who called it the turkey effect. Lots of carbs real quick, sap the energy in a body as everything goes into fat production. Meaning, she didn't do it often, but today she deserved it.

She could only imagine how it looked to Dwayne. He'd chosen to eat leftover roasted chicken, washed down with water.

He said not a word, but she would have sworn mirth danced in his eyes when she licked her fingers thoroughly before finally washing them at the sink. Already she felt a groaning lethargy spreading through her body.

"Bedtime."

"About time. I can't wait to get out of this suit." A drawled reminder of how he liked to sleep as he followed her to her bedroom.

Apparently, he'd forgotten her promise. She'd not been kidding about him taking the couch.

Planned her smirk of triumph when he beheld it. Only she was the one to frown as she realized something glaringly obvious. "You will not fit on that couch."

"I don't even know if it will support my weight," he said, eyeing it dubiously. "Does it serve any purpose?"

"It's elegant."

"Another word for useless."

"It's not useless."

"Prove it. Since it's just your size, why don't you sleep on it?"

"I will." Anything to make sure they didn't share that bed because the hardwood floor wouldn't be fair to either of them.

She glanced at her closet. Old house meant it didn't have a walk-in. "Turn around so I can change."

"Is this a coy way of asking me to peek?"

"Listen, Mr. Johnston—"

"Back to Johnston. I thought we'd gone past that to first names."

Her lips pinched. "This situation is untenable for us both."

"Speak for yourself. I'm actually finding it more amusing than expected."

"Well, I'm not. And your insistence on inappropriate remarks is begging to annoy. Can you control yourself? Do I need to request security?"

He stared at her, and his jaw stiffened. "I would never harm you."

"But it's okay to continually imply you're going to have sex with me?"

"Are you going to be uptight and claim sexual harassment? Because we both know it's only words. I ain't done nothing."

"Your words are offensive." But not in the way

she'd usually mean with any other client. When Dwayne spoke, her body heated.

"You want me to pretend you're not smokin' hot?" he asked as if surprised.

A blush almost heated her skin, but she bit her lip, the sharp pain stifling it. "I am your lawyer. Anything intimate between us would be highly unethical."

"You're single."

"No, I'm not."

He glanced around. "Yeah, you are."

It annoyed her that he'd pegged her personal life so easily. "Single by choice."

"Ditto and I ain't looking to change that. Truce?" He held out his hand.

"A truce meaning what?"

"I'll try and behave."

"Only try?"

The smile when it emerged had a dimple. "You are gorgeous. I might slip from time to time."

He was dangerous. So very, very dangerous, which was why she meant to only quickly shake his hand to agree. Only his fingers engulfed hers, and electricity zinged from him to her and back again.

Their startled gazes met.

Her breath caught.

He pulled away first, turning from her with a gruff, "I'm tired. Get changed. I won't look."

He was true to his word. She kept an eye on him

the entire time she stripped. He didn't budge once from his facedown position on the bed.

"Goodnight," she said.

"Turn off the light, would you?"

She moved to the switch by the door, and by the time she'd turned around, he was under the covers in her bed. Using her spare pillow.

The faint streetlight gave her enough to see her way to the bed to grab her pillow, and then she marched to her divan. Only to realize she needed a blanket, which led to more stomping as she grabbed one from the top shelf in her closet.

There was much fabric rustling, and a bit of grunting, as she did her best to get comfortable on the small couch. Every position failed. It was hard as a rock. Short. Narrow. She couldn't sleep on it.

She slid to the floor with her heap of blanket, but the old pine floor with the varnish worn away wasn't much better.

"The bed is big enough for two." The words were a gravelly reminder of who lay in it.

"I'm fine."

"Well, I'm not. All that tossing and turning is keeping me awake."

"Excuuuuuse me," she drawled. "Maybe you'd prefer to return to your cell?"

"What I'd like is for you to stop acting as if I'm about to ravage you like some uncontrollable beast if you join me in this bed."

"You're my client. It's not appropriate."

"I won't tell if you don't tell. Only the Devil himself will know, and approve."

Why had that whisper sounded closer? A sharp glance at the bed showed nothing but shadow.

When someone suddenly grabbed at her, lifting her from the floor, she yelped. "Put me down."

"I will," was his gruff reply. "In bed."

She hit the mattress and bounced then rocked as he slid in on the other side. She went to scramble off.

"Lie down," he ordered.

She would rather argue apparently, because her mouth opened, but before she could say a word, his voice whispered in her ear, "Or don't and I'll assume it's because you don't trust yourself beside me. It wouldn't be the first time a lady played hard to get in order to get me in her bed. Then, once she got me there, seduced me. Is that your plan, Kourtney?"

"I don't want you." Did he hear the lie as she hastily lay beside him?

He chuckled softly. "If you say so."

She did say so, which was why she had so many speeches prepared in her head, ready to blast him in the morning for his misogyny. Really, accusing her of being the one who'd molest him? She wasn't the one being charged with a crime.

She was...

Possibly sleeping? Or so she assumed, given she appeared to not be in her bed.

Instead, she stood in the crime scene of her latest case. The club, which had already reopened. Not that anyone noticed her ghostly presence. She stood as if invisible while people gyrated and moved around her.

I'm dreaming.

"What are you doing here?"

The rebuke had her turning to see a ghostly version of Dwayne. Even in her subconscious he scowled.

"How did you follow me?" he snapped.

"You're the one invading my dream!" she declared. "More like nightmare. I can't believe you've got me thinking about your case when I should be resting."

"You're asleep?"

"We both are. But apparently I can't keep myself from working." The quicker they proved his innocence, the faster they could go their separate ways.

Dwayne took a few steps farther into the club then pivoted and stared at the floor. "This is where they found me."

"I figured that." She'd seen the crime scene photos. "While there was no fluid in the immediate vicinity, you were drenched in it. Your palms were pressed to the floor, leaving marks. Knees too."

"As if I was dropped there."

"One possibility." She glanced overhead, unable to see what she was looking for between the strobing lights and the dark. "The cameras were supposed to be running, but no video has been located for that time frame."

"They record the events in this place?" he asked, sounding surprised.

"Given the potential for lawsuits and the fact roofies are getting too common, many businesses are trying to protect themselves. But in your case, hours of footage are conveniently missing. And you'll never guess when that starts."

"The same place as my memories end. At this ledge." He ran his finger on it.

"I figure one of two things happened next. You drank and were drugged right away, or you left and whatever happened occurred outside the club." She veered to eye the exit sign over a door to an alley.

"Would there be cameras in the alley?"

She turned a smile on him, never mind it was her own brain asking something smart. "Yes, but guess what?"

"They've been conveniently wiped as well."

"Correct, meaning you probably did go outside."

As if thinking it made it happen, she stood in the alley, the smell of garbage ripe, the air moist and chilly. The dream was too realistic.

Only a few people stood out here, pursed lips dragging on their vapes, while further down the dark corridor, the skunkier aroma of weed wafted.

"Why would you go into an alley?" she mused

aloud. She knew it was a mental fabrication. Obviously, her mind was working through some facts and trying to come up with answers.

"Only a few reasons and smoking ain't one of them."

"You were meeting someone. For sex?"

"It sure as hell wasn't to buy cookies."

"Depends on the cookie. That year there was a shortage from a certain brand and people got desperate." She'd mounted a defense for her client and, by the end of her presentation, had a certain cookie maker supplying her with enough boxes to last a year.

"If I went in the alley, it's because I followed a clue."

"You were looking for someone. Someone specific. Was it the missing girl?"

"No. Fuck no. The person I was looking for probably doesn't exist on any public registers."

"An illegal?" she asked.

"Put it this way, the person I was seeking belonged in Hell."

She caught the nuance. "You said that using the past tense."

"I could have used present too," he grumbled. "I don't know if they are here or there."

"There being?"

"Hell." He smirked as he said it. "She was, is, after all, a vampire in the Dark Lord's service."

She snorted. "Even in my dream you're crazy."

"Am I? You do realize that almost every single person in the world ends up in Hell when they die. Like me. And you."

"Speak for yourself. I've led a mostly clean life."

He laughed so hard she thought he'd cry. And when he started to recover, he eyed her and began laughing again.

Even in her imagination, she couldn't get the upper hand. "I fail to grasp the amusement."

"You're a lawyer."

"And a good person."

"No one is without sin. From the moment humans are born, it begins layering them. Filth covering them, although slowly at first. Not much sin when they are young, but it doesn't take long. People are inherently bad, especially greedy, grubby children."

Her lips pursed. "I might not be maternal, but even I drew the line at calling them names."

"You mistake me. I like children. Quite a bit. I am simply stating a fact. We are not without sin. Especially you. When the time comes, Heaven will reject you."

He sounded so sure, and this dream was turning strange. Since when did she believe in any kind of religion?

The door to the club opened suddenly, spilling noise and blinking lights as someone stumbled outside. It was a young man, his pants molding his body, his shirt open down to his navel. He had the weaving gait and unfocused gaze common in these places. He'd had a few too many to drink and no good sense left.

Only as the door closed and the distracting flashes disappeared did she realize the young man wasn't alone.

"The hidden figure." It was Dwayne who murmured it as he stared. "That night. I remember the lady in the head-to-toe silver cloak. She talked to me."

"She? You saw her face?" She ignored the inanity of asking her subconscious for an answer. At this point, she was making up facts. Nowhere in any reports did it mention anyone in a silver cloak. Who the heck even wore one to go dancing?

"I can see her and not, which is confusing." He frowned. "I remember green. Eyes. I think. Glowing. But there was something wrong with them."

"And now I know for sure this is crap. What a waste of time," she sighed, putting a hand to her head. Hopefully she'd wake up refreshed soon and tackle the real facts of the case.

He gripped her upper arms firmly and drew her on tiptoe. "What if I told you this was real?"

"I'd laugh. I'm not stupid. We're ghosts." She pointed out the obvious.

Dwayne pointed to the sign over the door. "What's it say?"

"Receiving, duh." Before she could add anything else, the young man who'd recently emerged staggered through them, but the one in the long cloak halted. Appeared to stare right at them.

Dwayne stepped in front of her. "What are you? What did you do to me?"

The deep cowl hid the features, and yet there was no denying the person saw and heard. The voice had a deep purr to it. "I can't believe you'd forget me so soon. And after the fun we had. You're quite the animal under the right circumstances."

"I would have never fucked you." His bluntness caused the robed figure to flinch.

"Says the man arrested for murder. I hear the humans have a strong case."

"No, they don't." Kourtney shoved forward. This was something she knew how to handle. "And once I find Ms. Lakely, they won't have one at all."

"Go ahead and try. Even if you find her, it won't matter once they find the next body."

"What body?" she asked.

"Yours." The robed figure flung an arm.

Before Kourtney could react, she was blinded by a dark fog. Almost a smoke with substance that cradled her and stole all breath. Literally. She gasped, her mouth opened wide, straining for something. Any ounce of air, only there was none in the darkness.

And then with an audible pop, as if a balloon exploded, light returned, as did sound and, best of all, oxygen, which she sucked in greedily. She heaved in breath after breath, calming her racing heart, taking stock of where she was.

With whom.

On *whom*…

She pushed on a solid chest and lifted her head to encounter the mocking smirk of her guest, who just had to drawl, "I knew you wouldn't be able to keep your hands off me."

10

THE RED IN Kourtney's cheeks aroused Dwayne. It shouldn't have. She was embarrassed, which led to her being livid. A live wire ready to zap him.

She was also beautiful and lying atop him, covering him quite thoroughly. While he'd actually kept on his shorts for sleep, the rest of him was bare and aware.

So was she.

Did she even realize she held her breath as she stared at him, her lips close enough he could have kissed them? What would happen if he closed that gap? Why she might even kiss him back. If she did, he knew what a pleasurable path that would follow.

But he'd long ago made himself a promise not to be distracted by fleeting fun. He'd done that before, for years, and it got him killed. He'd like to think he'd learned his lesson.

Still, there was something about having her near. The scent of her intoxicating. The moment ripe with possibility.

Her eyelids rested at half mast, heavy with arousal. Her lips were parted and moist.

The temptation was almost too much to bear. He needed to regain control of the situation. It started with reminding her to not trust the guy in the bed.

Dwayne grabbed her and rolled, narrowly avoiding the edge of the bed but managing to position her under him.

She gasped. "What are you doing?"

"You had a turn top. Now it's mine." He let some of his weight press on her, and she sucked in a breath.

"Get off me."

"Are you sure that's what you want? After all, you did start the groping."

"I moved in my sleep. An accident. Nothing more."

"It's okay to admit you like me." It wasn't actually. He could think of nothing worse. The reverse psychology failed him.

"I thought we talked about this."

"That was before you molested me in my sleep."

"I did not!" She shoved.

Some guys might have taken it a bit too far to prove they were stronger. Maybe even put a bit of fear into her because they could.

Dwayne didn't need to play those games. He rolled out of bed. "Rise and shine, my cuddly defender."

"Don't call it cuddling. I had a bad dream."

"It wasn't that bad."

"As if you'd know what I was dreaming."

"Did it involve a club followed by an alley with some weird chick in a robe?"

"You can't use the word chick. It's sexist."

"Then what should I say? Broad? Dame?"

"How about woman? Or, if unsure of gender, person?"

"You've got to be kidding me. You're going to get hung up on what to call the weird chick and ignore the fact you spirit walked with me?"

"A spirit what?"

"It's when you soul leaves your body and travels somewhere else."

She blinked. "That didn't happen."

"Yeah it did."

"If you're insisting it's true, then that must mean I'm still dreaming, and I can prove it. Hand me that book." She pointed past him to a stack on her dresser.

"Those don't look like research." The bare-chested dude on the cover was but a pale imitation of him. And a werewolf. As if those were sexy.

"If I'm dreaming, then I won't be able to read. It's a weird thing I learned from a television show."

"You're not dreaming," he said, handing it over and examining the next book in the pile. The cover had glowing eyes and the promise his bite would bring eternal pleasure. "What's it say?"

"*Taming Her Wolf.*"

"I told you you weren't dreaming."

She frowned. "I know the title. It could be I recited it from memory."

"Did you memorize the whole thing? Open it up and read at random."

Biting her lip, she cracked the book midway, and he could see her eyes moving, her lips tightening, until she slammed it shut. Her lips flattened. "It's impossible."

"Baby, there are so many things I could show you that would blow your mind." And that wasn't the only thing he'd like to blow. Then, before he gave in to temptation, he headed in the direction of her bathroom. He heard her scrambling to follow.

"I don't know how you did it, but we did not travel somewhere in my dream together. You made a lucky guess. Maybe I was talking in my sleep." She clung to the door frame, hanging on it as he rummaged under the sink for a spare toothbrush. He settled for his finger and some paste. He'd done worse in his unlife.

"Are you always this stupid, or am I just catching you at a lucky time?" He eyed her as he scrubbed.

"What you're implying is impossible. You can't really get inside my head."

"You're right. I can't. Nor do I invade dreams. What we did was go on a spirit walk."

"An out-of-body experience? I thought you needed to be floating in one of those sensory deprivation tanks to achieve the relaxation necessary."

"We had a little help from the Devil. At least I did. You apparently tagged along." When the Devil showed up the night before offering to help, he should have known there'd be a catch.

"We had an out-of-body experience," she stated aloud as if it would help her to believe. Perhaps it did because her next question made more sense. "How did we do it? Was it a drug? Did you inject me with something? Hypnotize me?"

"I had nothing to do with it. If you want someone to blame, then it would be the Dark Lord. He's the one who offered me aid that I might return to the scene of my last memory."

She crossed her arms. "You just can't help yourself, can you? You had me going along, believing the whole out-of-body thing, and then threw meeting the Devil in there. The Devil is a religious construct. He doesn't actually exist."

"I dare you to say that to his face," he muttered. She could deny the devil's existence all she liked. He couldn't forget it.

The moment Kourtney fell asleep the Devil had

appeared, wearing a onesie with a wide zipper, clown-sized feet, and a butt hatch. The bright red fabric showed off the yellow rubber ducks embroidered on it. The boy sleeping on his shoulder wore a matching set with the addition of a pacifier.

Dwayne had glanced at Kourtney. He expected her to open her eyes and harangue the Devil. She remained asleep.

"She won't be waking for a while. It doesn't take much to knock a human out," the Devil said.

That made him feel moderately more at ease. He slid from the bed and tucked the blankets around her. If she got cold, she might shake the spell, and then there would be some explaining to do.

"Got to admit I'm impressed. One day and in her bed already." The Devil beamed at him, and somehow the child didn't fall when the Dark Lord used both hands to clap.

"Nothing happened."

"Don't be modest. We both know you might be cold on the outside, but you run hot on the inside. Being in the clink must have been hard. But not as hard as you gave her the sausage I'll wager." The Devil winked.

"I didn't fuck her."

"The night is young. I say go for it."

"She's asleep."

"If she finds out, just lie and say she said yes. If

you want to really fuck with her, claim she orgasmed twice, screaming your name before you came."

The very idea had him shaking his head. "No thanks. I like my ladies conscious."

"But when they're awake they talk. Sometimes about their feelings." Lucifer made a moue of displeasure. "Can't they wait until after I've dealt with my needs? I mean who's more important here?" The Devil looked nervously at the ceiling then the window, as if waiting for something.

"Not all of us mind it when they open their mouths," Dwayne said.

"Don't get me wrong, a mouth stretched wide for a good knob polish is never wrong."

"That wasn't what I said."

"Ah yes, I should have guessed, given you're young and unfettered by the bounds of responsibility. How I long for the good old days when a lover would open her mouth wide for a hearty scream to let everyone in the vicinity know of your prowess as a lover, but it has its drawbacks once you're a parent. The strident decibel leads to children waking, which, in turn, creates a cock-blocking situation such as this one." The Devil gestured to the child sleeping against his shoulder.

"Was there a point to this visit?"

"Ah, the disrespect, how it soothes me to hear it, while angering me too. Not your brightest idea given I'm irritable from a lack of sleep and too much work. While you're not sinning and fornicating, or doing anything at all, I must deal with everything."

"Give me a task, Dark Lord, that I might ease your burden."

"Is it me, or did I hear you say 'pussy' at the end?"

More like Dwayne had thought it, which was dangerous in the presence of Hell's King. "I would never presume, mighty overlord."

"Maybe you aren't, but someone is presuming. Heaven has filed an injunction against Grim Dating, citing your crimes as reason to shut down operations. I think we have our *why* you were framed. But now we need proof about who. Have you made any progress?"

"Um, no. I haven't had much of a chance to do anything. I got out of jail today."

"And here you are wasting that freedom lying in bed, not even defiling the woman by your side." Lucifer huffed some smoke. "Absolutely appalling. I expected better debauchery from you."

"Sorry?"

"Argh. Must you make it worse by apologizing?" The Devil's agitation had the child stirring against his shoulder, rubbing his face. Lucifer froze. Eyed Dwayne with warning.

They both remained quiet until the child stopped moving again. Lucifer shifted the child's weight to a single arm then waved the other one before snapping his fingers. A sturdy crib with a hinged lid appeared. Not your standard infant furniture. The Devil held out his son, as if to admire him, which was why Dwayne didn't immediately realize the murmured words were directed at him.

"What?"

"I said, why aren't you out investigating?"

"How am I supposed to do that? I can't leave."

Lucifer guffawed. "You lazy fucker. Can't believe you're blaming the bracelet. Or haven't you realized how to fool it? Turn to smoke and leave it behind. Start your work. Be back before she wakes. No one will know."

"It's not the monitor that's the issue." It was, but a minor one in the grand scheme of things. "I can't smoke or even call a portal because my magic is still broken."

"Wait, what?" The Devil paused in the midst of placing the boy in the crib. "What do you mean broken?"

"Ever since I woke up in that club, my cloak isn't reacting like it should."

"And I'm finding this out now!" The statement held firm annoyance that Lucifer controlled as he lay the child down. He straightened and pulled the lid shut. Locked it. A snap of his fingers sent it away. He turned his fiery gaze on Dwayne. "Show me your cape."

Dwayne neared enough that Lucifer could grab at his cloak. The Dark Lord, after all, was the one who'd bonded it to his body and soul. If anyone could fix it…

A slight shiver went through the fabric and nothing else.

"This is unexpected," the Devil muttered. Not the most promising of words.

"Can you fix it?"

"I don't know." Lucifer sounded surprised. "I've never seen a case like yours before. Traces of the magic are there. I can almost touch them. However, it's not enough to use the cape as it's meant. Most curious and requiring more study."

"How long will that take?"

"How the fuck would I know? I will say, though, I'd be careful about doing anything dangerous while wearing flesh."

The Devil snapped his fingers, sending Dwayne back to the club. With Kourtney.

11

A CLEARING THROAT snapped Dwayne back to reality to see Kourtney eyeing him a little too intently. She looked annoyed.

Fuck, he'd zoned out again.

"Still waiting for an answer," she finally snapped.

"You wouldn't believe me if I told you."

"Try me."

"The Devil showed up in your bedroom and, when he found out I couldn't leave, snapped his fingers and sent my spirit to see the club."

That curled her lip. "That bullshit again? When is it time for the pitch to join the dark side? I'll tell you right now I am not signing any kind of contract in blood."

"I would never advise you to sell your soul. Live your life to the fullest and worry about negotiating when you're standing in front of him."

She blinked. "Did you forget to take some meds?"

If only he could show her. Swirl his cloak and disperse into a shadow. Then she'd have to believe him. Then she'd know he wasn't insane. But all he had were words. And not the right ones.

"I'm hungry." The problem with maintaining a corporeal form was the humanity that came with it. Such as a need to feed it. Even in Hell, he had to ensure he provided it with fuel. As a reaper—a creature of nothingness, only awareness—he didn't have to eat, but too long in that form caused other problems.

"I'm not your maid or cook."

"Then point me in the direction of your kitchen. I'll find something."

"We'll go together, or have you forgotten our matching bracelets?"

"As if I could forget the thing that had you spending the night in my arms." Just the right thing to say to get her to step to her closet and put on a robe that covered her neck to ankle.

"Any preferences for breakfast?" she asked, tightening the sash as if it were armor.

The corner of his lip lifted, and he said the craziest thing he could think of. Something he'd heard in a jest. "I would enjoy eating the unborn over some toast."

She didn't even crack a smile as she replied, "Eggs. Got it." Only to relent and say with an almost grin, "Do you think you're the first person to use that joke?"

"Just staying in character."

At that, she snorted and left the room. The soft beep by his feet reminded him to follow.

Kourtney's cooking wasn't quiet. She whirled dervish-like in the kitchen, flipping from stove, to fridge, to counter, and back. Not that he dared say a word while she cooked for him. Then again, who needed to talk with that wafting aroma? She didn't just make him some sunny-side-up eggs. She also made hash browns that popped out of the toaster oven a few seconds before she put the buttered toast on the plate. The sausage still sizzled when it hit the plate with the eggs.

She slid it onto the table, a masterpiece of food. His mouth watered. He did enjoy eating more on Earth than back home.

A second before he dug in, he looked over to see her raising a bottle of ketchup over it.

He yelled and swatted. The plastic thankfully bounced and didn't explode.

Neither did Kourtney. Very calmly, she eyed him and said, "You're lucky you didn't ruin my food."

"Damned right. Why would you put that swill on your food?" Ketchup had to be the vilest thing he'd ever unfortunately tasted.

"I like ketchup on my eggs and hash browns."

"No." He shook his head.

She cocked hers. "No? When did you get a say in how I eat my food?"

He opened his mouth to say something and realized there was no reply. He didn't have the right to decide what she liked. He sighed as he said, "Sorry."

"Wow, could you make it sound any less apologetic?"

He narrowed his gaze. "Are you always this combative in the morning?"

"Only when someone takes my ketchup away." She rose and grabbed the bottle, returned, and drizzled it over her food. She went to set it on the table, caught him staring, and, with a smirk, held it over her plate and squirted some more.

He shuddered. "Just for that alone, you're going to Hell." It never occurred to him that it was an insult until the bottle ended up aimed in his direction, the spout of it firing a stream of red.

He glanced down at the oozing gob on his chest. His bare chest. He'd only just managed to grab his pants and pull them on before he'd followed her.

Heat filled him when he caught her staring. Her cheeks reddened, and she ducked her head, the rapid shovel of food meaning she didn't have to say anything.

Was that how she wanted to play?

Fine.

He'd say nothing either! He proceeded to inhale his food, chewing the savory sausage. Dipping his bread in the juice to enjoy every last drop. When he finished, he glanced over to see her staring at him.

"You really enjoyed that breakfast."

"It was delicious."

"You didn't even add salt!" She made it sound like an accusation.

"Didn't need any. You cooked it perfectly."

She shuddered. "It's so bland without ketchup or something."

"It had just the right hint of salt. But if it makes you happy, I'll add a little pepper next time."

"There will be no next time," she grumbled, grabbing the plates and heading for her dishwasher.

"Is that the plan for today?" he asked, sitting back to enjoy the view of her bending over to put the dishes in the racks. "Are we trying to rid ourselves of these bracelets?"

"That is only part of it. We also need to follow up on clues."

"I didn't know we had any."

"We don't, which means we haven't talked to the right people yet."

"So who are you planning to grill?" He rose from the seat and snuck up behind her at the sink.

She finished washing her hands and turned around to find him right there. Ketchup level with her nose.

She blinked. "What the hell? Take a step back."

"I need something to wipe this with."

"You need a shower before we go anywhere."

"Ah yes, that vaunted half-hour."

"Try not to use all of it. I'd like to be out of here in the next thirty minutes, which means you need to shower and dress then get out of the bathroom so I can have a turn."

"Or we could really maximize our time and shower together." Sounded reasonable to him. But he knew she'd have a reply, and he almost smiled in anticipation.

She arched a brow. "Wow, I'm surprised you're advertising your inadequate stamina."

It took him a moment to grasp the insult. It was elegantly done. And a blow to his manhood. He gaped before blustering, "I am a fine lover."

"An efficiently quick one too. Good for you."

"I also can take my time."

"Not really interested. Which is why you get to shower alone." She shooed him. Waved her hands at a reaper and said, "Go. Shower."

A good thing she didn't follow. His balls had shrunk. She really wasn't impressed by him. He'd never encountered that before.

The anklet gave out a little warning beep when he closed the door between them. He heard her on the phone, faintly, "...he's going for his shower so don't freak out."

Apparently their thirty minutes started when she

called. He ran the shower and stepped in, barely noticing the chilly start.

He wasn't showing his best when a woman said, "That is a serious case of turtling, Johnston, and trust me, I've seen my share."

His hands dropped, and he whirled, the hot spray of the shower splatting off the back of his head. A woman stood at the far end of the tub. Which meant to say, about two feet away.

Given he didn't like surprises, he might have barked, "What the fuck, Bambi?"

Her lips curved. "Hello, Dwayne. Long time, no see."

Try when he was alive and banging every chick he could in the strip clubs. "Get out of my shower."

"I'll leave when I get some answers as to what the fuck is going on. Charged with murder. Sleeping with the company lawyer. Wasting time." Said so sweetly, it almost rotted the teeth.

"I didn't do fuck all on all counts. Kind of hard to investigate when I'm under house arrest and my magic doesn't work."

"So I heard. I have to wonder if your assailant knew what they were doing when they broke it or if it was an unexpected side effect."

"The Dark Lord said he'd never seen anything like it."

"As if my father would admit to a weakness in his

reaper design. He's always been so proud of your creation. Before the reapers, he used to have to collect the souls himself. He tried, apparently, handing the task off to demons, but they weren't the best at staying on task. Kind of like you. You seem distracted, Johnston."

"I just woke up. We're going to tackle the case today."

"The angels are trying to shut down my operation because of you. That can't be allowed."

"It would have been easier if you'd not shackled me with a human who knows nothing."

"Don't be so quick to discount Kourtney. She's smart."

"And in the dark investigating this case."

"Not for much longer."

"Meaning what?" A sudden fear gripped him. "Is she going to die?"

Her brow arched. "No idea, but I do know she's one of my father's special projects."

"Meaning?"

"That he's taken an interest in her. Why do you think she's the one working your case?"

"I would hope it's because she's the best."

"She is. But you have doubts?"

He turned off the water and grabbed a towel. "She is willfully blind to whatever doesn't fit her human worldview."

"She is skeptical, which, given her profession, is

rather to be expected. She deals with liars every day. She must pierce the layers to find the truth."

"She doesn't care about the truth, just winning."

"And how does one win? By knowing how to beat the situation," Bambi summarized.

"Speaking of Kourtney, she's probably going to wonder who I'm having a conversation with."

"Are you kidding? She is taking advantage of these fifteen minutes to do her own girl routine."

He frowned. "She said to hurry so she could use the shower."

"So you wouldn't know she was naked in another room, soaping that tight body. Wiggling into some clean panties."

He hadn't even thought about it until Bambi brought it up. Now all he could imagine was a soapy Kourtney.

He tied off the towel and peered into the steamy mirror. His jaw needed a shave. The foam he found under the sink had a floral scent and the razor a small pink handle.

Bambi perched on the vanity. "What's the plan for today?"

"Getting these bracelets off, and then, I don't know. She said something about finding some witnesses."

"I'm sure she knows what she's doing."

"I hope so." Because he definitely felt over his head.

12

It took a petition to another judge to declare the terms of the bail onerous and change them. It removed the ankle bracelets but kept the condition of them being together at all times intact. Not a perfect solution, but enough leeway that Kourtney could have a few minutes to herself without Dwayne looming in the background. She would enjoy that later when they weren't in the back seat of a car, heading for his office.

"I still don't see why we're wasting time at the agency," he said, not for the first time.

"Because I need to have access to some of the people you've been interacting with. Especially the clients. Could be someone you set up wasn't happy with the result."

"Then they should ask for a refund."

"How do I know you aren't hiding an ex-girlfriend at work who's pissed you're now sleeping with Sally from human resources."

"Sally is in accounting."

"You didn't deny a girlfriend," she pointed out.

"No point in denying the non-existent."

"Do you have any?"

"What?"

"Ex or current girlfriends?" A perfectly valid question yet it brought that small smile and his gaze softened.

"Such an interest in my sex life. Would you like a recommendation from past partners?"

"I'd rather kill the planet with batteries masturbating alone at home." A mature reply before she chose to ignore him and concentrate on her phone.

The sudden placement of his hand on her arm drew her attention, but she refused to look until he said, "Once again, I get to fucking apologize. I don't know why I'm a dick around you."

"Do you dislike me that much still?" She glanced at him to find him pensive.

"Dislike? On the contrary, I like you too much."

The admission charged the air between them. His eyes widened in shock. Her lips parted with nothing to say.

The car slowed to a stop, and the door opened. The moment shattered.

He offered his hand when she stepped out of the

car. She wrapped her fingers around his and ignored the jolt of awareness.

She needed space away from him and his damned virility. She also needed to buy a pack of C batteries.

She still remembered her first meeting and impression. Upon arriving, the building wasn't what she'd expected, yet at the same time was totally unsurprising. Chrome and mirrored windows. A sign featuring a cartoon reaper scythe through a heart. Not exactly the kind of image she'd gravitate toward if she were single, and yet—judging by the number of people moving around—the place was obviously doing well for itself.

She got the odd impression of the main floor having pockets of shadow all over with people sitting in the midst of them. A blink and they were gone, the vestibule brightly lit, the people just as vibrant.

From the moment they entered, Dwayne appeared more stoic than usual. His hands were shoved into his pockets, his shoulders pulled up in a hunch. She knew he wasn't in trouble given the company had hired her to defend him. Still, he didn't seem happy to be there.

The security guard waved a sippy bottle with some kind of bilious-colored liquid inside. At times she missed the days when it used to be a box of donuts instead of a milkshake of the most disgusting things.

"What floor is your office?" she asked.

"We can't go to my office."

"Why not?"

"Because it's pointless. It's just a desk."

"Then it won't take long to see it," she announced, heading for the elevators. A guess really but since there were large windows overlooking what appeared to be social rooms on the main level, she assumed the offices were at least one floor up.

"Nobody here would do anything," he grumbled, waiting by her side for the cab to return.

"Do you know the percentage of crimes that are committed by people we know?"

"Fuck your statistics." He rolled into the elevator and slouched against the back wall.

Her finger hovered over the button. "Two or three?"

"Two."

The doors closed. "Suck it up, princess," she said primly.

"Excuse me?"

"Stop it with the sulking. Your whining makes it appear like you're hiding something and don't want me to find it."

"Hardly. Search my desk as much as you like. That's not the problem."

"What is?"

The doors slid open, and a guy stood there, almost as if waiting. His tanned skin complemented his dark hair and wide smile. "Dwayne. I wondered when you'd roll into the office."

"Julio," her client mumbled.

Brown eyes perused her. "You should have told us you were bringing a lady friend. We would have tidied up."

"She's my lawyer.

"He knows that already," she snapped. "We met."

"Did we?" Julio played dumb. It probably wasn't that difficult.

Her lips turned into a flat line. "Kourtney Blake. I was hired by your company."

"Ah yes, the epically talented Ms. Blake. Did you know she's a crack shot?" The statement directed at Dwayne. "The Dark Lord couldn't stop singing her praises," Julio went on with a roll of his eyes despite Dwayne making slashing movements across his throat.

She stared at Julio. A second later she clued in. "I should have known you'd work off a script. Is it part of the employee handbook when you're hired? Add 'Dark Lord' to every other sentence to stick within the theme?"

Julio's brow wrinkled. "What the fuck?"

Dwayne surged forward. "Give me a second," he said as he swung his arm around Julio and drew him a few paces away, where he whispered.

She didn't hear anything, but it concerned her. No doubt in part given how Julio peered at her in surprise during it.

Since they were having a reunion and probably getting their stories straight, she stepped farther into… Well, she wasn't sure what to call that room. It most closely resembled a call center, with a few added features. A pool table in the far corner with a few arcade-style games. Kitchenette area with a buffet and a long counter lined with stools. There was even a corner with couches and a few massage tables set up.

And then there was the room itself, partitioned into waist-high sections. Some had desks with monitors and chairs that could roll. Others had tables with chairs opposite. Then there were another few built like pods, and inside… She squinted. People napping?

It almost made her want to be an employee. Except she'd need walls and her own bathroom. A woman did have her standards after all.

She strode toward a desk, only to have Dwayne suddenly appear by her side. "Where are you going?"

"To check out your workspace."

"How do you know which one is mine?"

She halted by the desk with absolutely nothing on it. "Tell me I'm wrong."

"Must you always be right?" he grumbled.

"Yes." She sat in his chair, conscious he loomed

over her. Oddly enough, she didn't feel frightened or intimidated. With some clients, she would never dare make herself vulnerable, and yet, there was something about Dwayne. Something solid. Like a rock.

She glanced at him and saved a joke for later. She didn't enjoy spontaneity, so she always prepared an arsenal. "Walk me through your job."

"I sit. I read files. I make recommendations."

"What kind of recs?" she asked, opening the drawers to find one paper clip, a pencil, and an unopened pack of business cards with the cute cartoon reaper on the front.

"The kind that result in good matches."

"Because you're an expert." Less question and more a statement.

"I look for locations that will provide the perfect date," he specified.

"Doesn't seem all that hard."

"It's not. Like I told you. Boring."

"Do you have anything to do with the couples themselves?"

"Only if the date goes wrong."

"Meaning?"

"Sometimes I intervene if two subjects are incompatible."

"Isn't that counterintuitive to the adage opposites attract?"

"Yes, but sometimes they also kill each other," was his morbid reply.

"Was your mother's name Morticia?" she muttered, bending down to see if there was anything under the desk, more to avoid him for a second than anything. She'd almost straightened when she saw it.

She plucked the bug free, and as she rose, she held out the bug until he frowned.

"What is that?"

She rolled her eyes. "Way to be subtle. It's a listening device."

"Listening to what?"

She pointed at him, and he looked so flabbergasted she laughed.

"I fail to see the humor," was his stiff-lipped reply.

"Because you can't see your face. Do you have an envelope?"

"Do I look like the type?"

"I have one." Someone from the next cubicle over leaned in, her expression avid. "Can you check my desk for a bug too?" The young woman with the lightly freckled face smiled.

Dwayne growled from behind. "This is none of your business, Ariel."

"If we're being bugged, we need to know," Ariel insisted.

"She has a point," Kourtney added to be helpful.

"I know. I am not stupid. First, though, we need

to take this to the commander."

"How ominous," Kourtney declared, but she rose, the envelope in her hand.

Before she could take more than a few steps, there was a commotion and Julio exclaimed, "You. Again. How many times do you have to be told we'll call you? Don't call us."

She whirled to see a man all in white, which might have appeared odd on some, especially out of the tropics, but he carried it well. The linen shirt was buttoned over his evenly tanned skin, a hint of golden kiss, and tucked into his slim-fitting white khakis. On his feet were white loafers. The only thing not completely white were his shades. Silver framed and lensed.

"Who is that?" she asked.

"A holier-than-thou pain in the ass," was Dwayne's reply. "Hold on while I handle this."

As if she'd stand back. If this appeared as if it would get ugly, she'd yank her client out of there. He wouldn't appreciate getting tossed back in jail.

As she neared, she realized Dwayne and Julio had been joined by a woman who towered over Kourtney. The three of them confronted the man with the golden curls and smiled.

"What an honor to have you all greeting me. I feel special," he said.

"Hope that feeling holds you all the way out the door, Raphael. Get out." Dwayne pointed.

"But I've just arrived," Raphael protested.

"This floor is for employees only," Julio stated, arms crossed.

"Then hire me," Raphael teased.

"You know the commander said your kind ain't welcome," Julio said.

"And what kind is that, Julio?" Raphael said, but his gaze flickered to her. "Well hello there. You're new."

Dwayne shifted to block the view. "Not a client, Raphael."

"Even better. Your services are expensive for what amounts to merely a coital exchange."

"Not a whore either," Dwayne barked. "She's my lawyer."

"Yours, not mine. And in a fun-sized package. Stand aside so I can say hello," Raphael purred.

"No need. Hello." She fixed Raphael with her firmest glare. "And goodbye." She turned and snared Dwayne's arm on the way.

At first, he tensed as if he'd refuse to follow. But he eased, and she felt him shadowing her back as she aimed for... She didn't know where she was going until he whispered, "Stairs straight ahead unless you want to go past him to the elevators."

Stairs it was.

They shoved through the door, the exit spray painted over with the words, *Escape*. Glancing at the flight going down, she did debate it. What did she really think she'd accomplish here? She didn't have the slightest idea what to look for. Only luck had led to her finding a bug.

The reminder had her eyeing the envelope. A spy might mean her gut hadn't led her astray. What happened to Dwayne might be connected to his company.

Rival dating agency trying to take them out? It sounded like a very B movie with horrible dialogue, which meant it would make for a compelling argument if needed in court.

The stairs going up wouldn't get any easier for waiting, but she did wish she'd not worn her three-inch heels in an attempt to not feel so short. Vanity was about to kill her feet.

She'd taken three steps when she felt herself lifted, literally. An arm snaked around her waist and then jostled her up the stairs as a show-off took them two at a time.

"I am capable of climbing stairs," she retorted, but not until he'd reached the top and set her down.

"Until you twist an ankle. Those are an accident waiting to happen." He pointed to her feet.

"They make my legs look longer."

He snorted. "No, they don't. And ain't nothing wrong with your legs." He froze as if he'd not meant to speak aloud, and then he whirled and grabbed for the door. "Let's go see if the commander is in."

What a dichotomy of a man. One minute, flirting

to the point of being obnoxious, and the next, saying something genuine and acting as if he'd committed a cardinal sin.

Just as she moved to follow, the fire alarm went off, a strident scream of sound that had Dwayne grimacing more than usual. He tucked her close before people began streaming out the door, most muttering, "There's no fire," and "It's not as if we can die."

They really took their roleplay seriously. Rather than follow them down in the crush of people, all taller than her, he turned her upwards.

"Where are we going?"

"The roof."

"Isn't that in the wrong direction?"

"Trust me when I say it will be a nicer spot to wait for the all clear."

When she hesitated, he lifted her, and she might have protested except, glancing down, she saw the slow march of bodies and wasn't interested in joining them. Might as well be on the roof where the air was fresh.

They emerged onto a flat pebbled deck strewn with a hodgepodge of chairs. Mostly office ones, a few looking worse for wear.

"I didn't know you smoked," she said, glancing down at the bucket with ash and butts.

"Not anymore."

"Good for you. Smoking kills."

"All bad choices kill. It's a matter of whether it is worth the cost." He glanced at her, and his shoulders rolled.

"Why did you want to come to the roof? If there's a fire, shouldn't we be on the street?"

"There's no fire. And it's much nicer up here where the air is fresh."

Her nose wrinkled. "I can smell exhaust and something that might be burning meat."

"It gives the smoke flavor."

"I'd prefer that of the forest."

"Wouldn't know. I never went camping. My parents' idea of a family vacation was dropping us at my aunt's while they hit a casino. Closest I got to a forest was about ten trees clustered in a city park." An admission that had him dropping his head, as if ashamed.

"If it makes you feel better, we stayed at home for the holiday. I was the kid who did her homework and got ahead during every school break."

That drew his gaze. "Strict parents?"

She nodded.

"Whereas mine never gave much of a shit. I mean they did in their own way, but I didn't make it easy for them. I wasn't good in school. I got caught smoking in the boys' room. Getting drunk under the bleachers. Got expelled at one point before I graduated." He shrugged. "A family will only tolerate so much."

"You don't get along with them?"

"They're all gone now."

"Mine lives across the country. We talk a few times a year."

"Sorry."

"Why? Can't miss what I never had," she admitted, which wasn't something she did often. She had to wonder where this candor came from.

"Ever wonder if we're missing out?"

She shrugged. "Family is who you make it."

"Guess so. The crew from the guild"—he shuffled and glanced down—"I've known most of them since I joined. They're kind of like family in the sense they'd have my back."

"But?"

"I don't want to come home to them every day and talk."

The strange turn brought a frown. "What are you trying to say?"

"Nothing." The scowl dropped into place. "The alarm seems to have stopped. We can probably go back inside."

He strode away, and for a moment, she held out a hand as if to stop him. She wanted to ask if there was someone he liked talking to, because it occurred to her he talked an awful lot to her. And she replied, and not just as a lawyer with her client.

But as a woman interested in the man.

13

WHAT THE FUCK was wrong with him? Dwayne had been off kilter since waking up in that club and even more so since he'd met Kourtney.

Discussing his feelings. Almost admitting his obsession with her. His desire…

Weak. Stupid. Totally not the right time or person. But he couldn't escape her. He sensed her presence at his back as they went back down the stairs. This time he let her walk. Not the easiest. He kind of enjoyed carrying her around.

Too many things about her felt right and good.

The stairwell wasn't completely empty as a few reapers stood in the landings, clustered and whispering. They spotted him, then Kourtney, and hushed. A few grinned knowingly. No way to hide they'd come down from the roof together.

They assumed the wrong thing. Never mind the fact he'd almost given in and kissed her a few times.

He'd held back, fifty percent convinced she'd slap, bite, or knee him if he tried. The other half of him worried even more what would happen if she kissed him back.

"Is the commander inside?" he asked as he held open the door to the top floor.

"Nah," said Maurice. "Which is part of the reason why his angelicness got so pissy and *accidentally*"—he did an air quote—"set off the alarm."

"Raphael never was the type who liked to be told no," Dwayne muttered.

"What's this I hear about you finding a bug?" Maurice asked. "Who planted it?"

"Dunno." Dwayne shrugged.

"Don't you have camera footage?" Kourtney interjected. "An office this size surely has surveillance, if only to ensure no possibility of being accused of impropriety."

Dwayne glanced up while Maurice stared at his feet. Shit. One of them had to answer. "No cameras. Commander don't like them." A simple excuse.

She let out a sound that might have been a swear word. A very rude one. "Meaning liability is a possibility. Does the company have insurance for that kind of accusation?"

"Uh," was Dwayne's brilliant reply.

Maurice stepped away, saying, "Gotta go. Do. Stuff. Something." He waved as he walked away.

She shook her head. "I can see why your company needs a lawyer. So many policies will have to be updated."

"I don't think the boss will approve cameras." He didn't bother to hide his doubt. Kourtney didn't know who worked in this building, the clients they served. Yes, their glamours would pass muster in most cases, even if caught on video, but if they slipped and turned it off… Or what if a reaper disappeared in plain sight?

They already knew if a reaper drew their cloak and called on magic to walk through the nether place they literally disappeared into thin air. Cameras were a bad idea.

So he distracted her with a stupid one. "Dark Lord doesn't believe in using technology when the old ways work."

"I saw the computers," she said as they stepped back into the stairwell.

"The Dark Lord hasn't yet found a magic to replicate how smart they are."

"Got lots of magic happening in the office?" She arched a brow as she kept pace going down the stairs.

"All the time." The truth and yet she laughed, a lovely, low sound that made him shiver. His cloak rippled too.

"The company might want to implement a fraternization rule."

"I wasn't talking about that kind of magic." Amazing how she never once believed anything he said.

"Why would that guy pull the fire alarm? Is he a client?"

"Was."

"Did he fire Grim Dating, or did you drop him?"

"A bit of both. It didn't work out." For Raphael or Michael.

Kourtney frowned. "Has he caused other problems?"

"Never anything you could prove. His sort is very careful."

"Sort being?"

"Religious. Worships Elyon, his strict rules, and Heaven."

"Who is Elyon?"

"I am not getting into that." His turn to shake his head. Explaining Elyon was God's most current appellation would lead to talking about Lucifer, which she'd scoff.

"Cameras will alleviate any more attempts to cause trouble."

"Doubtful. I'll even wager right now that had we footage of today, it would still appear an accident." The angels were too sly to get caught. How to explain the angels had been causing all kinds of subtle trouble since they lost the wager and Grim Dating was allowed to stay in business. Angels might give the appearance of losing with grace, but they'd get their revenge.

"Do you have many problems with disgruntled clients?"

"Nothing we can't handle." But that might not last. Raphael and Michael were of the elite echelon and part of the group trying to get Grim shut down. As if that weren't problem enough, to make matters worse, both had been roundly rejected by women. First, Raphael—convinced of his own superiority—was dissed by a human. Then it was Michael's turn. He was a pompous angelic ass who got his vanity handed to him by a witch.

The angels hadn't yet declared war, just played their annoying pranks. It made Dwayne want to hit something.

"You're glowering again," she remarked

"Smiling inside," was his sarcastic reply.

She slowed as they went past the middle floor where he rarely worked. "Where are you going?"

"Anywhere but here."

"Who says I'm done?"

He could have argued. Asked. Done many things that didn't involve grabbing and tossing her over his shoulder.

Some women might have screamed and punched him. Her voice dropped to frosty with a chance of emasculation. "Your caveman tendencies are getting to be tiresome."

"Stop arguing so much all the time."

"This isn't an argument. This is you making decisions for me, and I won't have it."

He reached the last step and flipped Kourtney to her feet. "Too bad. So sad."

"You are really starting to piss me off," she hotly exclaimed.

"Only starting?" He leaned closer. "Maybe I need to try harder."

"Are you trying to intimidate me by pretending we're going to kiss?"

"Who says I'm pretending?" he drawled.

She stood close to him, not backing down, never fleeing in fear. Her chin lifted. "You won't kiss me. You threaten. But you won't."

"What makes you think you know me?"

"I don't, and you don't know me very well either." She grabbed his cheeks and yanked him close to her.

She kissed him!

Thoroughly. With tongue. And heat.

Arousal arrived instantly. He burned for her—

She stepped away. "There you go. Fixed that threat for you. Care to make any more?"

He blinked at her. She'd called his bluff in the most pleasurable way and now smirked in triumph. "You weren't supposed to do that."

"Don't make promises you can't keep." She gave

him a saucy wink before stepping through the door to the main level.

It was a good minute before he could follow. He expected to see her waiting for the elevator to return to his desk, only she stood impatiently by the doors, phone in hand, barely glancing up when he appeared.

Could she truly be so unaffected?

"About time. I was beginning to think it would take you forever to tug one off."

His jaw dropped, and she laughed. Where was his serious lawyer? Who was this woman with the ability to jest ribaldly?

"Don't look so gobsmacked. Did you forget where I worked for the last ten years? I've heard it all."

"Did you kiss them too?" he snapped.

Her chin lifted. "No." Just the one word and yet it hit him hard.

She'd only ever kissed him.

Fuck.

What did it mean?

It meant he followed her fast-moving, tiny body out the door as their Town Car pulled to the curb.

"Where to next?" he asked. He wagered she'd already decided on somewhere. Otherwise she'd have never left.

"We need to hit a forensic lab and have them examine the microphone."

Give possible evidence of Hell's existence on Earth to humans? "I know a place," he quickly exclaimed. "It's company approved," he added before she could refuse.

Helga—their driver—knew exactly where to go when he told her they needed to visit the OAB.

Thankfully Kourtney didn't ask too many questions because he had no idea how to explain the Office for Abnormal Beings. From the outside it appeared as a regular building, no sign to announce the bureau's presence.

Kourtney stopped looking at her phone long enough to question. "This is the place? Is it a secret lab or something?"

"Private lab and investigators. They can have this scanned and give us the results within a day or two."

She insisted on joining him, but given the bureau maintained a legit appearance on the main floor, all she saw was a dingy reception with a few plastic chairs and a woman sitting behind a battered desk with cat-eye glasses perched low on her nose. Her gray hair was pinned into a bouffant. Lips, with cracked red lipstick, parted. "Can I help you?"

"Yeah." He leaned forward. "Grim Dating needs a rush job on this." He gestured for the microphone.

The receptionist held up a finger. She leaned down and placed a glass box on her desk. "Place the object inside."

Brows raised, Kourtney dropped the envelope in.

When the lid closed, it shimmered for a second. A protection spell in case the device was still active.

The receptionist grabbed the glass box, turned, and placed it on a pile of identical boxes. "We'll call when it's done."

His lawyer frowned. "Aren't you going to give us a receipt for it?"

Red lips pursed. "Of course." The receipt was scrawled on a piece of paper that had Kourtney muttering under her breath as they exited.

"We are going to have to find you a place that takes chain of custody a little more seriously."

"Given we found it and not the cops, it won't really matter," he pointed out.

"True. Here's to hoping whoever planted the bug can help your case."

Their car had to park farther up the street. When they emerged, brake lights on it lit. Helga had seen them. Rather than make her do a U-turn, they walked toward it.

"It's going to rain," he announced.

Kourtney glanced upward, and a fat drop hit the tip of her nose.

He couldn't have stopped himself if he tried. He kissed it. And then froze. He blamed that stupid embrace of earlier. She'd changed the dynamic between them in doing that.

Her startled gaze met his, and he waited for her reaction.

She didn't recoil. Her lips parted in invitation.

Oh, hell yeah. He'd readied to dip for a kiss when a car drove through a puddle by the sidewalk and soaked him, and only him.

She stepped away and gaped. "Are you okay?"

"Do I look okay?" was his snarled retort. A soggy crotch didn't make him feel romantic, and neither did the dirty water running in his eye.

They reached the car, and she slid in first. Dry as a bone. He sulked in the corner, hiding somewhat in the faint shadow of his robe. Not that she noticed, busy again on her phone.

Stupid thing. She always had her face in it. Modern technology was to blame for a lack of manners.

He didn't even realize he'd snatched it and fired it out the window until she screeched, "What did you do?"

"It slipped."

Her eyes widened. "You're fucking nuts." The expletive exploded from her lips.

"You work too hard."

"Trying to save your ass."

"You're not going to find the truth of the matter on the internet."

"I wasn't on the internet, smarty pants. I was actually setting up an interview with the bartender for that night."

"He wouldn't have seen anything."

159

"Says you."

"Yeah, says me."

She twiddled her thumbs but not for long before tapping on the partition for their driver. When it lowered, he caught sight of Helga behind the wheel.

"I need a new phone," his lawyer stated.

"Rogers or Bell?" asked Helga.

"Rogers. I have an account." She glared at him. "Although this will be invoiced to your company. Paying for destroyed property isn't part of the deal."

"You just can't stand not having it in your hands can you."

"Can too."

"No, you can't." He remembered the look of addiction. Booze, drugs, and women for him. Work and her cell phone were hers.

"Is there a point to this argument?"

"Just that forcing a clue is a waste of time. We'll know what we're meant to know in due time."

"That's some hokey crap."

"It might surprise you to know I believe in fate."

"It's not fate if you do stupid shit and it comes back to bite you."

"It's the coming back part I'm counting on. Someone went through a lot of trouble to frame me. It stands to reason if they see it failing, they'll try something else."

"If at first you don't succeed," she muttered.

"That's not a bad theory. If it's correct, then we should lay a trap."

He snorted. "And lace it with cheese?"

"This is not a cartoon and we're not hunting rats."

"I wouldn't be so sure. This is more the work of a higher functioning demon." He spoke the truth, not caring if she believed him.

She must have become immune. She didn't even remark on his accusation. "I think tracing the source of that fake blood will lead us to the culprit. It can't be that common."

"Put it in daylight and I'll bet it disappears." It had occurred to him after the fact that there was one kind of blood that might not appear human. "Vampire blood has unusual properties." Unlike that of a demon, which had a tendency of dissolving once it left a body.

"Are you changing your argument from the Dark Lord did it to a vampire? It's got a less Satanic bent that might be easier to sell."

"If it was a vampire's blood, then they're probably still alive. Exsanguination weakens but doesn't kill. And had they died, there would have been a puddle of sludge." Really gross. He'd only ever seen it once in his reaping life when he came to fetch the soul of the human the vampire killed.

As the leech drained the last of the blood, the woman's husband appeared, injured but alive, and rammed a broken chair leg through the vampire's chest. The vampire exploded into chunks and gore. It went everywhere, including the face and hair of the recently dead wife. She screamed all the way to Hell, and since it was vampire stained, Dwayne had to get his robes cleaned.

Despite his hatred of the phone, it was quickly replaced. However, to his surprise, when Kourtney returned to the car, she kept it in her briefcase. She also unbuttoned her blouse and removed the clip to her hair, fluffing it.

"Why do you appear as if you're primping for a date?" Was she preparing to kiss him again?

"I have an interview with the bartender."

Apparently, this wasn't about him. His mood turned sour. "Good looking, is he?" Wait, not sour, jealous!

"I have no interest in his looks. This is because Mr. Tom Newton wants me to meet him at the Mission Church. According to my search, the only thing happening around that time is a meeting for Sex Addicts Anonymous in the church basement."

Her reasoning filtered quickly. "You're going to tempt a pervert?"

"I am going to get answers."

A fine plan until they arrived at the church to see the flashing lights. Shoving their way through the crowd, she found a police officer who was able to tell them that a man had died. His body was found in the church's bathroom, strangled with his own belt. A sexcapade gone wrong, of course.

One guess as to who the body belonged to. There went a possible clue. But of more concern to Dwayne? According to the reaper wandering the scene, Tom Newton's soul was nowhere to be found.

14

THE BARTENDER WAS dead under suspicious circumstances. With no ideas, they returned to Kourtney's house, where she fired up a lasagna she kept in the freezer, mostly ignoring her guest as they ate but constantly aware of him. Why did she have to go and kiss Dwayne?

It was dumb. So very, very dumb. What had she hoped to accomplish? Other than make a fool of herself because it backfired. Her awareness of him proved distracting.

Yet, despite his previous words, he didn't appear affected, or in the mood to talk. At times, when she glanced over at him, she would have sworn he was covered in a shadow, staring at her pensively, almost jerking when he got caught.

She'd stepped over a line kissing him. She'd have

to recuse herself, unless she could prove herself competent.

After dinner, she closed herself in her office, meaning he could snoop through her house. Even leave without her knowing. It made her twitchy. She kept glancing at her door, wondering what he was doing. Even stood a few times to go check.

Eventually, he did appear, only to say, "Going to bed in the room you have at the front of the house with the green wallpaper." He meant her guest room.

He didn't ask. Didn't wait for a reply. Simply left.

She should have been pleased he was starting to show her some respect. Instead, she couldn't help a spurt of annoyance. Had the flirting this entire time been a sham?

It shouldn't have mattered. Yet, at the same time, it miffed.

Since she couldn't concentrate, she went to bed, where she lay on her comforter, staring at the ceiling.

Was Dwayne asleep? Had he stripped naked to do so?

Being aware a man slept down the hall was the most ridiculously girly thing ever. He was a client.

A criminal.

A man of many moods, yet she didn't lock her door. Dwayne might be acerbic to the core, slightly oddball, but a killer? She didn't think so.

Eventually, she dropped into a restless slumber

where she startled at every noise. In an old house there was always something creaking, but the groan of a house shifting held a much different pitch than that of a door swinging open on stiff hinges.

She immediately sat up and began the speech she'd prepared while battling her insomnia. "Mr. Johnston, this is really most inappropriate for you to be..." Her words trailed as the faint light from the hall illuminated a strange shape. Not tall enough to be Dwayne. Nor the right shape. Could it be a draft had opened the door and the shadows played tricks?

A believable scenario until a pair of eyes suddenly glowed red.

Being a rational person, Kourtney knew this had to be a dream. Being a smart person, she yelled, just in case it wasn't. "Intruder Scenario Five!" Because single women, especially those working with criminals, had the best home security systems.

An alarm wailed, lights came on, and she had a moment to curse her sudden imagination as Dwayne appeared in the doorway.

"What's going on? Where's the attack?" He wore only his boxers and nothing else, hands spread, ready to defend.

"Cancel," she yelled, first to silence the alarm and to ensure law enforcement weren't called. Good thing she'd built in a sixty-second delay in case of a false launch.

He rubbed his face. "What the fuck was that about?"

"I thought I saw someone in my bedroom," she sheepishly admitted.

"Where?"

Her nose wrinkled. "Where you're standing."

He took in a deep breath, held it, and let it out. His brow furrowed. "Stay there for a second." He moved into her room and into the closet.

"There's no one here," she exclaimed. "I'm sorry, I didn't mean to wake you up."

He emerged, ignoring her to check out her bathroom next. She got out of bed and started to say—

Nothing, because he wasn't in there?

She stepped in far enough to look behind the door and inside the shower. Where had he gone? When she emerged, she frowned at the empty bedroom.

"Dwayne?" She peered around, even ducked to look under the bed before heading out into the hall.

He called her from behind. "Still here."

She whirled, stalked back into the bedroom, and frowned. "You weren't there a second ago."

"Sure, I was. Checking the window. Must have not seen me because of the curtains." He smiled weakly as he shoved at the sheer fabric. "They're painted shut."

"Yes, they are, and no one is here. I am sorry I woke you."

"I wasn't sleeping," was his gruff reply.

"Why not? Is the bed not comfortable?"

"Bed is fine. Just missing one thing."

"What?" was her soft reply, caught by the intensity of his gaze.

"You." An admission followed by a kiss.

Earlier, she'd caught him by surprise. He'd kissed her, but obviously held back. Not anymore.

His hands cupped her jaw, cradling her face as he explored her mouth. His bare chest rubbed against the thin fabric of her top. She'd not worn a bra tonight, which he quickly discovered when the top was removed.

She pressed her torso against his, a sweet friction that only intensified the awareness. Her breasts tightened into buds, forming hard protruding nubs that rubbed against his chest. The drag of the tips on coarse hair sent shivers through her. Her legs weakened, and she sagged against him. His arms were there to catch, tightening and holding her firmly against him.

Between her legs, she throbbed. She pressed against his thigh, letting her legs spread that she might rub herself against him. She ground her sex against his muscled leg, up and down, gasping in his mouth, shivering in arousal.

He expanded his sensual exploration by dragging his lips across her jawline to the sensitive lobe of her ear. He tugged it with his teeth, and a deep moan slipped from her. As he sucked the flesh, his hands skimmed down the bare flesh of her upper body, hooking on the elastic of her sleep pants, tugging them downward, forcing her to shift from her grinding enough that the loose fabric puddled at her feet.

As the cooler bedroom air hit her butt, she had a random thought that maybe she should slow down.

Stop.

Stop now when she finally tasted the passion people boasted about?

She'd rather be fired.

Her turn to grab his cheeks and deepen the kiss, her tongue thrusting into his mouth to taste him and feel the vibration of his groan. His hands cupped the fullness of her bottom and brought her back to his leg, meaning her clit got direct contact from the firm muscle. Friction from the short hairs. She shuddered at the pleasure.

She gripped his muscled shoulders as she rode him and only vaguely noticed she dug her nails into him. His fault. The arousal proved too intent. Her need too great.

She lost his thigh, only to have it replaced by his hand. Deft fingers toyed with her slick and swollen nub. A cry slipped past her lips as he stroked her, rubbing her clit while thrusting his fingers into her. Something she could squeeze. Back and forth. In and out. He brought her to the edge.

And then his hand was gone, replaced by what she really wanted. The tip of him butted, and she moaned, lifting a leg to drape it around his hip. He slid in, but the angle was a bit too much.

She gasped when he cupped her by the ass and lifted her. She groaned when he then dropped her onto his cock.

Deep. So deep. And thick. It stretched, it pushed, it felt great. Her legs locked around him. Her arms twined his neck. They kissed as he lightly bounced her, just enough to really put pressure in the right spot. Every time it hit, she squeezed around his thick shaft. Again. Again. Her cries and breaths were ragged.

Her nails bit into his flesh. Her body coiled. Tense. Taut. With a hoarse cry, she burst. Orgasmed with a pulsing bliss that had her keening.

He joined her with a soft whisper of her name.

And even when their breathing slowed, he didn't move away. He remained buried inside her as he carried her to bed. Wrapped around her as she fell asleep. When she woke before him and wiggled, he was ready to go again. Ready to slide into the heat of her and make her realize last night wasn't a fluke.

When he dropped to his knees in the shower, she saw his pleasure had many facets.

Morning dawned, and despite wanting to stay in bed, she rolled out of it, pulling on track pants and shirt.

"Where you going?" he grumbled, shoving his face into the pillow.

"I need coffee."

A smile hovered on her lips as she went downstairs. It lasted until she got to her kitchen and saw the door standing wide open. She frowned. It had been locked the night before.

Dawn spilled over the threshold, bright and inviting. She glanced upstairs then immediately mentally chastised herself. Since when did she need to call on a man? She had her phone in her robe pocket. She kept one hand on it as she padded close enough to glance outside.

Someone stood in her yard, and she couldn't help but exclaim, "What are you doing here?"

15

LYING IN BED, Dwayne laced his hands behind his head. Waking up beside a woman proved a nicer than expected experience. Heck, sleeping beside someone was novel in and of itself.

He'd had no interest in a relationship until now. Meeting Kourtney had changed his perspective. Rather than wanting to avoid her after the night they spent, he found himself more eager than ever to spend time with her.

Only she wasn't in the kitchen. The coffee pot not even started. The counters pristine without any hints of breakfast. Not that he cared about food. The heart in his solid body almost stopped as he noted a door to the outside looming open.

Why would she have gone into her yard? A few reasons quickly occurred. Yoga. Feeding the birds or other wildlife. Fetching something from a garden. Eggs from some hens?

None of them fit the woman he knew. Perhaps he panicked for nothing and yet he still leaped across the room, flinging himself outside into the brightest of sunshine, showing off the pristine landscaping fenced in with six-foot white pickets. The gray patio stones were dry, a good sign since no blood marred them. The two chairs flanking a table were empty.

Kourtney was gone.

And judging by the phone sitting on the ground? Not by choice.

He knelt by the cell. The screen was cracked. His cloak lightly shimmered, vibrating as Dwayne tried to force it to help him look past the mundane to see what kind of traces were left behind.

For a moment, his view tilted, and he saw a filter of auras. Dull for stone. Vibrant shades of green for the living plants and trees. An orange-yellow that he knew was Kourtney's and—

His vision flipped off, but he still had his other senses. His nose didn't detect any brimstone or rot. Rather, the air held a crisp sweetness to it that pleased the senses.

He paced the patio, looking for anything he might have missed. A speckle of blood. A scrap of fabric. He didn't find any signs of violence other than the dropped phone. He also didn't sense any other reapers nearby. He would have known. Death left a trace.

If she lived, then it meant someone dared to take her.

Who? Mostly importantly, where?

His cloak ruffled, and for just a moment, he could have sworn he felt her, the tug of her soul calling to him.

Thump.

"He's in the yard!" someone yelled.

It would appear he had company. Dwayne turned just as the police officers spilled from the kitchen door into the yard. More came in through the gate attached to the side of the house. They arrived in full riot gear, guns out, the one in the lead barking, "Hands over your head."

Arguing didn't seem prudent. Not with his cloak malfunctioning and his body very susceptible to damage.

Dropping to his knees, he hands laced over his crown while annoyance brought a scowl to his face. They wasted his time when he should be looking for Kourtney.

He barely listened as a female officer read him his rights and cuffed him. Only as a duo marched him out of the house did he ask, "Why am I being arrested?"

"They'll tell you at the station," said an older,

grizzled cop whose belly strained the vest he'd worn over it.

"Why not tell me now?" Dwayne argued.

"You know why," snapped the old dick.

The female officer was the one to explain. "Assault and kidnapping."

"Of whom? Was Ms. Lakely found? Because if she has, then she'll just need one look at me to prove you've got the wrong guy."

"Don't play dumb," snapped the old dick as he shoved Dwayne into the back of the car. "A witness saw you when they were walking their dog. They reported how you attacked Ms. Blake in the yard."

"Why would I attack my own lawyer?"

"Because you're a psycho who should have never been let out of jail. Consider your bail revoked." The female officer couldn't contain her glee.

"Surely you can see there's holes in that story. If I attacked Kourtney, then where's her body?" Dwayne pointed out the obvious flaw.

"You must have stashed it somewhere nearby. And you better hope she's alive, or they'll be upgrading those charges to murder."

"Is your entire fucking department incompetent?" Probably not the best thing he could have said.

"Don't bother trying to argue with me. You can do that with the detective at the station."

The door slammed shut, and once the cops got in

the car, they proceeded to ignore him, which annoyed. But not as much as being arrested again. Kourtney needed him, and he'd gotten stuck dealing with idiots.

"Why are you joyriding in the back of a cop car instead of doing what I demanded?" boomed the Devil, startling him.

A glance at the cops showed them paying no attention to the fact the Dark Lord had joined him in the back seat. "What exactly would you suggest I do? My cloak is still broken."

"About that..." The Devil shifted in his seat, leaning enough to show he carried a baby in his arms. Her curly locks of hair were ebony with a sheen of red. He had creamy skin and a single tooth. "Meet Jujube."

"She your kid?"

"A chip off the old demon she is." Lucifer bounced her on his knee, and the child grinned. "And lucky for you, I think she can help us."

"How is a baby going to help?" He couldn't hide his skepticism.

"Because she's a special baby, aren't you, snookums?" Lucifer rubbed his nose against the child's. He smiled, the baby laughed, and outside, the sky darkened. The Devil frowned. "We need to make this quick. The wife is in a bit of a mood lately."

Everyone in Hell was aware Mother Nature hadn't been herself since her children were born. The climate activists blamed it on pollution.

"Do what quick? Because you haven't actually said what we need to do."

"Fix your cloak, of course. Hand it over." The Devil held out his hand, wiggling his fingers with impatience.

With nothing to lose, Dwayne grabbed the material and draped it over the Dark Lord's palm. He just about yanked it back as the Devil then proceeded to wipe the baby's drool-riddled mouth with it.

"What are you…" His voice trailed off as his cloak shivered, and for a second, magic coursed through him. Filled him. Then fizzled.

He could have bellowed in frustration.

The baby squealed and grabbed his cloak with two chubby fists. With a single tooth, and lots of gums, she began chomping on it.

Yum. Yum. Yum.

Goo. Gooey. Gross.

Dwayne tried to not wince at the amount of slobber being soaked into the fabric. His cape shivered and kept trembling even when the Devil said, "Okay, Jujube, that's enough." He yanked the cape free, handing the soggy mess back to Dwayne. The baby's face screwed, readying to yell.

"Don't you dare," Lucifer warned. "Your mother is not in the mood to have you throwing a tantrum."

Jujube opened her mouth, and her eyes lit with flames. Defiant and did the Devil chastise her?

He beamed. "Such a bad girl."

The baby gurgled, and the devil held her close. "That's my girl."

"I thought I was your girl." The woman that suddenly appeared between them drew unmanly squeaks from them both, but Jujube giggled.

Lucifer managed a high-pitched, "Wench. What a surprise."

Mother Nature appeared radiant, wearing a summer frock with a flower motif, her hair coiled atop her head and escaping in wisps. She looked like spring beside her husband, dressed emo-style in black turtleneck and khakis. It was only if one looked close that the embroidered mouths, open in screams, appeared in the fabric of her dress.

"You know what's a surprise?" Mother Nature said, bopping the baby's nose with a finger. "It's finding out my husband is taking our daughter for a ride in a police cruiser with a criminal."

"Actually, he's a reaper."

"Even worse," she declared. "Really, Luc, I thought we spoke about not unduly influencing the children to choose one side over the other."

"I swear I wasn't."

"Then what possible reason could you have for subjecting our daughter to a stranger?" She cast Dwayne a glare that would have shriveled him if he were a plant. She huffed and turned her laser stare back on the Devil.

He wanted to confess. To hold out his wet cloak

and say it wasn't his idea to let the baby goober all over it. The Devil whispered for his ears alone, *Shhh.*

"Give me my daughter." Mother Nature held out her hands, and there was a reluctance in Lucifer's face that he quickly masked. He began to pry the baby free, but she fussed.

"Da."

"It's ma time." He deposited the child with Gaia. "About time that you did your fair share, wench. Are you finally done being a lazy ass?"

"Feeling better than ever, which means you don't have to worry about caring for the children. I'll take care of them." Said on an ominous note before Mother Nature blinked out of sight with the baby in her arms.

"Fucking hell. Why can't I have a few decades of happy wife, happy life? And a better question, why do I keep getting pulled back? It's always the same shit. Which means I gotta go get dirty." The Devil eyed him. "I trust you can handle things from here."

"Handle how? I'm still broken."

"Not for long. I figured out how to break the spell."

"Using baby spit?" he asked dubiously.

"It gives me the lube needed to do this." The Devil put his hands on the toggles of the cloak, burning palms that heated them to the point Dwayne's mouth opened wide on a silent scream.

Pain and yet it was more than agony. His body

bowed, and his cloak expanded, then contracted, and turned to smoke before becoming the warm shadow he'd missed.

The reaper was back, and so were his powers.

Which meant, when the cops finally glanced into the backseat to check on him, they found it empty.

16

KOURTNEY SHOULD HAVE RUN back into her house the moment she saw Lakely in her yard. The rational part of her knew a supposed victim of a murder and a definite missing person wouldn't be skulking around her begonias for any good reason. But apparently sex had addled her wits.

When the woman wrung her hands and said, "Are you Ms. Blake?" she replied, "I am. You're Ms. Lakely, correct?" At the head bobbing, she added, "People are looking for you."

"Which is the problem," Lakely muttered.

A rapid visual check of the other woman showed no signs of abuse. She appeared clean, unharmed, and alone. "Listen, whatever trouble you're in, I'm sure we can find a solution to it. Once you prove to the police you are alive."

"I hear they arrested Dwayne."

"You know Dwayne?" For a brief moment, jealousy flared.

"We met the night he was found covered in blood." Lakely hung her head, hiding her expression. "I warned him not to get involved."

"He doesn't remember anything about that evening."

"It was best he forget," she said softly.

"You drugged him?" She couldn't help the surprise in her tone.

"I didn't have a choice."

"Is someone threatening you?" Kourtney stepped closer to reassure the young woman.

"There will be trouble if anyone finds out."

"Finds out what? Come with me and we can talk about it. If you're scared, the police can provide protection."

"No police." The words emerged flat from behind the veil of hair hanging in Lakely's face.

Kourtney wanted to shake the woman because Lakely's presence meant she could get the charges dropped against Dwayne. "How about we just let them know you're alive and safe?"

"If we tell them that, then it will ruin everything." The coy smile set off alarm bells.

"I'm going inside."

"No, you're not." A hand shot out and gripped her wrist. "You're coming with me."

Lakely might be bigger, but one good scream—

All the breath whooshed from Kourtney as wings suddenly sprouted from Lakely's back. Big. Fucking. Wings. White, with heavy streaks gray. They flexed.

Kourtney finally squeaked, "What the hell are you?"

"What am I? Seriously?" muttered Lakely. "I hate atheists."

Tugging at the grip on her wrist proved futile, and she couldn't escape the glowing silver rope that appeared in Lakely's other hand. She soon found her upper body bound, the loose end tied around Lakely's waist.

In the distance, she heard sirens and had a moment to wonder if rescue was on the way. Hopefully they were also sending a helicopter, as Kourtney discovered those wings actually worked.

Lakely sprang into the air and extended the feathery appendages. Half expecting to fall back to the ground, Kourtney closed her eyes. When they didn't hit solid Earth, but the rush of air blew past her cheeks, she kept them screwed tight. Flying should be done inside a plane, with an engine and a steward offering drinks.

If this was a nightmare, then someone should explain it to her stomach. It rolled as the bird woman banked, their flight a noisy thing of wind and flapping wings. Surely this wasn't real?

This could be like the dream she had with

Dwayne where she was at the club. Only he'd implied it had really happened.

What if she really were flying in the air with a giant bird lady?

After a while, when she realized Lakely's plan wasn't to drop her and make her into a smudge on the sidewalk, she ventured, "Where are you taking me?" Though she really wanted to ask, what are you?

"You'll see," was the cryptic reply.

They were probably less than five minutes in the sky, but miles from where they'd started, before her stomach dropped as they lost altitude. She swallowed hard against the fear and uttered a sob of relief as they hit the ground, alive.

The moment Lakely released her, she stumbled away, opening her eyes finally to see she stood in an overgrown field. Was this where she'd die? How many murder mysteries started in a similar setting?

She began to run, only to trip, her still bound arms unable to break her fall. Breath whooshed out of her at the impact.

"Get up." Snapped impatiently.

"I can't. Hands tied, remember?" was her frustrated reply.

A yank on the rope binding her put her back on her feet, an amused Lakely cocking her head. "That wasn't too bright."

"I had to try," she mumbled.

"Let's go. She's waiting."

"Who's waiting?"

"You'll soon find out."

Exiting the field, she noted a house that hadn't seen better days in a while, the paint on its siding peeled and faded. Their destination was around the back, where a cellar door showed signs of recent repair.

Before it could be opened and Kourtney thrust inside to probably die—because good things didn't happen in abandoned cellars in the country—her captor exclaimed, "How did you find us?"

"I am the finder of souls." The deepness of the statement sent a shiver.

The rope leash slackened, and Kourtney whirled in time to see a shadow taking shape in the moonlight. Not just any shape.

"Dwayne?"

Her querying note drew his cold gaze. The icy blue momentarily softened at the sight of her. She could have sworn she heard him whisper even though his lips didn't move. *You're safe. I'm here.*

A guy thing to say but she allowed it in this instance. Because either this was a dream or she'd stumbled into some hokey shit.

Given how real it all felt, and the fact she could read the logo on her captor's shirt—Nobody's Angel —she was definitely awake. What had she gotten involved with? And damn this freaking rope. She wiggled her shoulders as her kidnapper stalked toward Dwayne.

"You shouldn't be here."

"What did you think would happen when you took Kourtney?" Dwayne stepped closer, and she would have sworn a cloak made of shadows rippled at his back.

"Wait a second…" Lakely glanced between them before muttering, "Oh poop on a stick. You're sleeping with her?"

"I think the more important thing is, why the fuck did you kidnap her?" He stood still, but the shadows around him didn't. They swooped and swirled but never strayed far from his body. Hypnotic if watched for too long.

"Because I needed fresh blood." She shrugged.

"They blamed me for her disappearance," he growled, and his cape shivered with him.

"As I'd planned. I will add this is your fault. I wouldn't have had to kidnap your lawyer if you'd gone back to Hell. The entire Grim Dating sham was supposed to shut down." Her lips tilted downward, in an expression of discontent.

"Is that why you framed me? Heaven wanted to shut us down and couldn't think of a better way?" Dwayne asked.

She laughed, the tinkle of bells, silvery and light. "As if Heaven would do anything. The credit is all mine."

"Good to know." As he spoke, a gleaming axe appeared in his hand.

What the hell? What was happening? Apparently, she spoke aloud, but it wasn't Dwayne that answered.

"Don't tell me you don't know?" Lakely gaped over her shoulder then laughed at Kourtney's expression. "My God, who art in Heaven, you don't, do you?"

"I know enough to see I'm being played. What's happening here?" Kourtney grumbled.

A smile crossed the other woman's lips. "I am obviously Heaven's emissary."

She couldn't help a dubious, "You're an angel? Aren't angels supposed to be nice?"

Lakely's lip curled. "The ones still behind the gates are. I'm the kind that gets special dispensation because of the work I do to keep their hands clean."

"And he is, what? Some kind of demon ghost?" She said it mockingly while, at the same time, wondering. Dwyane appeared human enough. Felt alive. Not once had she suspected he was anything other than a man.

"Your lover is a reaper. Bringer of death. Taker of souls. He is the Dark Lord's pet."

She glanced at him, wondering if he'd deny it, but his head tilted. "You're wasting time. Why?"

It was Kourtney who figured it out. "She's not here alone."

"I know," was his reply. "I also know she can't come out in daylight, which means we've got hours to waste."

"Are you implying her companion is—"

"A vampire. The one I've been seeking," he said, taking the weirdness of the situation up a notch.

"We love each other," declared Lakely.

A vampire and an angel, it boggled the mind.

"Love?" He snorted. "She's been here less than a week."

Kourtney understood his skepticism. Could you fall in love with someone that quickly?

"We knew the moment we met that we were meant for each other," Lakely declared. "But you know the rules between our kind. What would happen if we were caught? I had no choice when you came sniffing around. You would have told Lucifer, and he would have tattled to my Lord, who art in Heaven. Hallowed be Elyon. It would have been over for us. The archangels would have come for me."

"And your brilliant plan to prevent it was to let people think Dwayne killed you?" blurted Kourtney.

"It worked." A roll of Lakely's shoulders matched her nonchalance. "The reaper sent to find Noel was kept out of the way. Everyone was focused on the blood and not me or Noel. As a bonus, I was told if it shut down Grim Dating I wouldn't be hunted."

"Who told you that?" Dwayne demanded.

The query clamped Lakely's lips. "No one. And

I've said too much." She held out her hand, and in it appeared a sword, dull gray, like the edges of her wings. "You should have gone back to Hell when you had a chance."

"Is this where you kill Dwayne? And then what? Claim self-defense?" Kourtney exclaimed.

"I won't have to say anything, because we both know a dead reaper can't tell tales. And as for you... Like I said, Noel is hungry. No one will ever know what happened to you."

"I'll know." It appeared Kourtney still had the capacity to be surprised because she squeaked as a man stepped out of literally nowhere, wearing calf-high leather boots with tan khakis tucked into them. A dark shirt was buttoned up the front and paired with a leather coat. The hat screamed Indiana Jones, but rather than a whip by his side, he had a little boy with solemn eyes, which, for a moment, appeared to reflect red.

"Dark Lord." Dwayne dipped as if the guy were royalty.

Lakely made a moue of disgust. "So you are the Fallen One."

"The one and only Lucifer Baphomet, and you'd better fix that disrespectful tone, young lady."

The title sank in. Kourtney gasped. "Are you the devil?"

The head spun too many degrees for comfort.

"Depends. Did your mother claim I was your daddy?"

"No."

"Then, yes, I am *the* Lucifer, Dark Lord, purveyor of sin, maker of witches, father of many demons, and so forth and so on." He flourished a hand. The baby chose that moment to burp.

He glared. "Wait your fucking turn."

"Don't talk to him like that," Kourtney huffed.

"Or what?" The Devil arched a brow. "You do realize Junior did that on purpose to manipulate the situation."

"I highly doubt that. He's a child."

"He's my son." Flatly said. "And already using some of my best tricks. But your impertinence when it comes to my parenting isn't the issue here. You." He pointed a finger at Lakely. "You've been a bad girl."

The angel lifted her chin. "If I did something wrong, then I shall confess and do penance to receive absolution."

"Not this time. Your crimes cannot be ignored anymore," Lucifer declared.

"Bad," agreed his son, clapping his hands.

"It's not a crime to love," Lakely stated hotly.

"It is if you've got them tied up like a rabid dog," Lucifer stated, and Kourtney's breath sucked in as his eyes lit as if on fire.

"Noel loves me."

"What do you say we ask her?" The Devil snapped his fingers. The yard outside the house went from morning sunshine to night. "That's better. Can't have Noel roasting like a marshmallow, can we? Vampire skin is so sensitive to those UV rays."

Nervous glances at the cellar door betrayed Lakely. "I should be the one to fetch her."

"You mean kill her before she tells us the truth?" The Devil smirked. "Do you really think I'm that stupid?"

As Lucifer spoke, Dwayne and his shadow slipped into the basement.

Lakely fidgeted. "How did you find out I had her?"

"Not easily, I'll admit. My progeny tend to not always be visible to me on this plane. A most annoying problem I've yet to fix. It doesn't help when someone uses concealment magic to further confound."

The child at the Devil's hip slid down and toddled toward Lakely. She flinched when he reached for her. Even pulled back her foot as if to kick.

"I wouldn't do that if I were you," was the Devil's soft warning.

Dwayne reappeared, a thin woman following at his back, her expression stern. It narrowed as she perceived Lakely then turned to relief as she saw the

Devil. She dipped to a knee. "I failed you, Dark Lord."

"You did, but I forgive you. Mostly because you led me to this treasure. It's been awhile since I've had the pleasure of dragging a fallen angel to Hell."

"I'm not fallen," Lakely insisted. "I've been forgiven my trespasses."

"Not this time you haven't. I can see the guilt staining you," the Devil declared.

"Dirty," agreed his son.

Lakely finally looked frightened.

"Let me kill her for you, my lord," hissed the vampire.

"But I love you," insisted Lakely.

"You knocked me out with magic and locked me away."

"I brought you blood."

"And almost killed me too! Draining me almost dry."

"So we could be together. I had no choice when he sent a hunter to find you." Lakely had the nerve to toss an annoyed glare at Dwayne.

"What do you know of the bartender's death?" he asked, unperturbed.

"What bartender?" was Lakely's reply. The innocence wasn't feigned.

It was the Devil who cocked his head and stated, "She's been wiped. There are holes in her memories. Large ones."

"Are not," Lakely hotly huffed.

"Oh, fallen one, you have no idea just how sorely you've been used. And now forsaken."

"My father, who art in Heaven, would never abandon me."

"Then call him. I'll wait." The Devil crossed his arms, and his boy mimicked.

Kourtney found herself shifting closer to Dwayne, who'd come to stand by her. For all that he had his secrets, she felt safe around him. Which was kind of ironic given he was a purveyor of death.

The fallen angel lifted her head to the sky, clasped her hands, prayed silently with her eyes shut, and her lips moving. Then aloud, crying out, raising her arms, only to stamp her foot. "This isn't fair. I am an angel of Heaven."

"Not anymore." Lucifer smiled, a terrifying thing that brought a shiver.

Dwayne tucked Kourtney even closer, his robe swirling warmly around her frame.

Rather than cower in defeat, Lakely lifted her chin. "I wish to negotiate the terms of my surrender."

"You do realize I could have Noel rip out your throat," the Devil said, waving at the vampire, who smiled with both fangs.

Still the angel didn't look afraid. "Kill me and you won't find out my secrets."

"What secrets? Your mind is like Swiss cheese."

"Not everything was stored in my head." She tapped her temple. "I kept a diary."

"And you wish to trade it for a lighter sentence?"

Lakely nodded. "To ensure I get a fair deal, I want Ms. Blake to help me negotiate the terms." She pointed at Kourtney.

"No." Dwayne surged between them, wanting to protect her.

Yet, she'd rather speak for herself. She stepped forward, ignoring the shadow fabric rippling to her side. "I'll help, but on one condition. First, you come with me to the police station and clear Dwayne's name."

"If we must." Lakely uttered a long-suffering sigh.

"Yes, we must. How else will you be able to resume your life in the city?"

"I have put in the time to build up a reputation. And my apartment is prime real estate," Lakely murmured aloud.

"Forget going back. It will never will happen," the devil said with a snicker.

Kourtney eyed him. "Excuse me, but I'm having a private conversation with my client."

"I will not excuse you. She and I have business." Lucifer declared.

"And we'll get to it after we handle the police."

The Devil huffed. "Who says I'm giving you permission to do a pitstop?"

"Ms. Lakely is a key witness in the charges

against Dwayne, who is in your employ I believe?" She glanced at Dwayne, and he nodded. "Meaning it is in your best interests to allow me to clear up his legal troubles before our next bit of business."

"Now you're talking my language." The Devil rubbed his hands, and his Mini Me copied him as he said, "Let's make a deal."

Before Dwayne had a chance to talk to Kourtney, she, the devil, and the fallen angel went off to handle the cops. Even Noel went as backup in case Lakely tried to run.

Kourtney didn't say a word to him. Not one.

As for the devil, his simple command was, "Stay here."

It left him with only a few options.

Option A, vigilante justice, where he sent the unworthy of Heaven to Hell. With B, he'd report in to the commander and wait for his next Grim assignment. Or he could go with the crazy C and find out if they had any leads on the listening device.

He paid a visit to the OAB and was sent to their technical department in the basement. Upon entering, he took in at a glance the rows of counters lining the room and, above them, a massive web. The mistress of that domain, Marsha—an arachnid from the Hell dimension, given special dispensation to work on Earth—didn't even bat one of her dozens of eyes. She twisted in her web, her many legs moving in tandem until she could face him.

Her mandibles clacked as she hissed, *You were the one to bring the device. Where did you find it?*

"What, no hello?"

Click. Clack. *Important.*

"It was under my desk at the office. Why, what's wrong?" He'd had few dealings with arachnids, but he knew they weren't usually this terse and agitated.

Not from Earth.

"Hell then?"

Click.

"Heaven?"

Clack.

"Somewhere else?" He knew there were other planes, just not readily accessible.

Alien.

Now there was a word to give even a reaper pause.

The news bugged him. It bugged the commander. It might have bugged the Dark Lord himself if he'd taken the time to answer his call.

What the heck was happening in Hell? Would Kourtney return? Forgive him?

As the hours passed, he sulked at the office, a

hulking shadowy presence until Julio barked, "Would you go home already?"

Home.

Yes. Good plan.

With his magic back, he stepped into the portal that appeared at his desire and walked out into Kourtney's place, where he waited.

Waited until the front door opened, and she sauntered in, tossing her briefcase onto the table.

"If it isn't the Honorable Kourtney, home at last."

She didn't appear surprised to see him. But she did have questions. "A reaper, eh?"

"I tried to tell you."

She grimaced. "You did."

"Does it help if I say the souls I collect aren't from people I killed?"

"Nice to know the guy I slept with isn't a murderer. But you're also not human anymore," Kourtney pointed out.

"In some respects, no, I'm not." For a moment, he let his cloak appear, a shadowy presence that swirled and drew her gaze. Yet she didn't appear afraid. "The magic imbued upon me at my death hasn't change the fact that I'm still a man." A man who felt. Felt more than he'd ever imagined when around her.

"You do realize now that the charges have been dropped you're free to go home."

"What if I wanted to stay?" The moment hung heavy with possibility. Would she reject him?

"Here? With me?" She finally sounded surprised.

"I want to be with you." The blunt truth.

"We'd need a cohabitation agreement."

"That's not very romantic," he said, sliding close enough his cloak could swirl around her feet.

Her lips quirked. "You going to hold me in contempt?"

"Most definitely," he purred, sliding his hands around her waist.

"What's my punishment?"

"Extreme pleasure. The kind that will make you scream. And squirm." His hand slid between their bodies, only barely noticing the business suit she'd managed to don since he last saw her. It didn't take much to rip. When he touched her between the thighs, she was already wet and ready.

Her head went back as she gripped his shoulders.

He stroked her. Dipping and teasing, the slickness of her sex driving his thrusting fingers. When he couldn't stand it anymore, he sat her on the chair he'd vacated and knelt between her legs. The taste of her was the paradise he'd thought lost to him. Her soft cries the sweetest music.

And when he slid into her, he knew one thing for certain. He wanted to be with her forever.

EPILOGUE

A FEW WEEKS LATER, *at a cottage she rented for a weekend...*

A mist hung slightly above the water, obscuring the opposite side of the lake. The surface proved still. Not even a ripple from a dancing bug.

The orange glow lightened the fog to their east, the brightness of it fighting against the shadow that clung to the land.

Kourtney tucked closer to Dwayne, her head under his chin, his robe wrapped around them both. The chair, Adirondack she called it, with its deep seating, easily held them both. She nestled in his lap, snug and warm. As to why they were awake at the crack of dawn?

He had to show her the miracle he'd discovered the previous day.

"It's coming," he whispered.

"Not yet, but soon," was her saucy reply.

He hugged her tight enough to make her squeak, and then he snuggled her as dawn burst into existence, lighting the world in the most radiant colors. Bathing him in its rays. Its warmth turning the lake into a vision of color that stole his breath.

As beautiful as it was, though, the best thing of all was nestled right there in his arms.

Kourtney tilted her face to him and said, more than a little pleased, "I knew you were a hillbilly at heart."

Which he'd never suspected. However, Kourtney had a feeling and insisted they leave the city that he might experience nature. Apparently, she knew him better than he knew himself. "I think the correct term, counselor, is outdoorsman."

"You own too much plaid now for that."

"Not my fault. When I discussed with my friends our plans to vacation at a cottage, I was told I needed to have some."

"There's some, and then there's your wardrobe. You even got plaid boxers."

He grinned. "Flannel boxers."

"You got me a plaid nightie!"

"Also flannel, with matching robe and slippers."

To which she laughed, a sound for him and him alone. She might be a serious lawyer in the daytime, whipping Grim Dating's legal issues into shape—and brushing up on folklore to deal with her new clients —but at night, and on the weekends, she was his reason for smiling. The thing he'd been missing all his life and unlife.

"Fuck me but I love you," he said. "Now and always."

LUCIFER TURNED OFF THE SCREEN BEFORE THE NEW lovers got to the good part. Look at him being all mature and stuff. Not watching people fuck without their knowledge.

He didn't have to. Of late he was getting all kinds of sex.

Too much sex.

Gaia had gone from too tired to overwound. As in bouncing off the walls, too much energy.

Thinking she'd created some new plant with medicative properties, he'd asked for a hit. She'd laughed and just said life was making her feel good. There might have been the hint of lie in there, but he forgot about it when her lips wrapped around his knob.

All was right in his world again. His kingdom thriving. His minions getting hooked up and popping out more babies than ever.

Even on Earth, things were going well for once.

So why did he get the feeling the pendulum was about to rapidly swing the other way?

The missive flew out of a tube and hit his desk, the container cracking open, the scroll inside rolling free.

He didn't want to read it.

Didn't want to see what it said.

That smacked of cowardice. He opened it. And cursed softly so she wouldn't hear him, even as he knew he wouldn't be able to hide it.

The ninth ring had just been lost.

Julio had his feet resting on the desk when the angel walked in. The commander had decided to take a short holiday with his new girlfriend and left him in charge. Not a hard thing to handle really. All he had to do was ensure everybody showed up and did their jobs.

However, no one left instructions on what to do when the angel he rescued showed up in front of his desk with hands clasped and said softly, "I need to find out how angel babies are made."

Was it wrong for him to say, "Sure. Shall we have the demonstration on the desk or in a bed?"

Is Grim Dating about to make another match with Julio? Or will the taboos between their kind keep them apart? Find out in Knocking on Helen's Door.

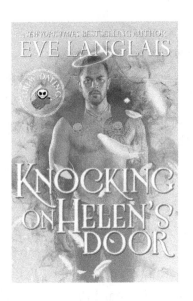

For more stories please see http://www.EveLanglais.com

Newsletter: http://evelanglais.com/newrelease